THE WRANGLERS

THE WRANGLERS

Will Cook

Chivers Press • G.K. Hall & Co.
Bath, England   Thorndike, Maine USA

This Large Print edition is published by Chivers Press, England, and by G.K. Hall & Co., USA.

Published in 1999 in the U.K. by arrangement with Golden West Literary Agency.

Published in 1999 in the U.S. by arrangement with Golden West Literary Agency.

U.K. Hardcover ISBN 0–7540–3539–5 (Chivers Large Print)
U.K. Softcover ISBN 0–7540–3540–9 (Camden Large Print)
U.S. Softcover ISBN 0–7838–0356–7 (Nightingale Series Edition)

The text of this Large Print edition is unabridged.
Other aspects of the book may vary from the original edition.

Set in 16 pt. New Times Roman.

Printed in Great Britain on acid-free paper.

British Library Cataloguing in Publication Data available

Library of Congress Cataloging-in-Publication Data

Cook, Will.
    The wranglers / Will Cook.
        p.   cm.
    ISBN 0–7838–0356–7 (lg. print : sc : alk. paper)
    1. Large type books.   I. Title.
    [PS3553.O5547W73   1999]
    813'.54—dc21   98–33783

CHAPTER ONE

As soon as the fall cattle drive was over Old Man Guthrie called out the names of the men he was laying off, and they went to Lordsburg to get their final pay. Guthrie had no use at all for credit slips or checks; he paid in cash, on the hotel porch at six o'clock, and he hadn't changed this procedure for twenty years.

Ben Clayton was a horse wrangler. He always came last in line to get his own accumulated pay and Charlie Gannon's. They were close, these two. Clayton was a very young man, twenty, or maybe a little more—he didn't really know himself. Five years before he'd been a stray up from Texas and he'd asked Guthrie for a job. At the time Guthrie recalled that he hadn't wanted to put him on, but he had because Charlie Gannon had asked him to.

Mighty funny, the way those two got on right from the start: this was the old man's thought as he counted out the money in two piles.

'Where's Charlie?' Guthrie asked. 'Puttin' up the horses?'

'Yep,' Ben Clayton said. His hair was the color of old straw, and there was a splatter of freckles across the bridge of his short nose. He had his man's growth, tall, lanky, quick as a cat, and at times as unpredictable.

1

'That's yours on the left there,' Guthrie said. 'I raised you ten dollars, like I said I would.' Since the paying was over, he tipped back his chair and looked at Ben Clayton. 'Five years now I've laid off, paid off. Do you handle all of Charlie's money?'

'He'll be along,' Ben said, still smiling. He looked up and down the street, remeasuring it as a confinement of the fun he'd anticipated for four months. 'Don't this town ever change?'

'What's to change?' Guthrie asked.

'I don't know,' Ben Clayton said. 'But I remember it as lookin' better than this.'

'You shouldn't do that. A thing is always a disappointment when you think about it too much. You and Charlie wintering out in town?'

'I guess,' Clayton said. Then he laughed again. 'I guess we haven't changed much either.'

It was dusk of a quiet day, yet heat lay strong between the suncracked adobe buildings. Clayton's glance picked out a man who walked slowly toward the hotel, and he stepped off the porch to meet him.

He handed Charlie Gannon his pay, and said, 'I expected you sooner.'

'What's the hurry?' Gannon asked. 'We've got all winter.'

He was older than Ben Clayton, some fourteen years older, and more settled in his ways. They stood there together and watched

2

the Tombstone stage making up in front of the depot. Passengers came out and got in and Ben said, 'Where do people go when they take a stage?'

Gannon shrugged. 'I wouldn't know, couldn't care,' he said. He was a little shorter than Ben Clayton, but heavier, much more solidly put together, as though his Maker had meant him to be strong and durable for a particularly rough life. Gannon's hair was thick and dark and curly and needed a barber's attention. His trade was apparent from the way he dressed. Over his faded jeans he wore a pair of batwing chaps, standard garb for a bronc buster. A scarred and torn brush jacket fit him a little too tightly at the shoulders; it was rain-shrunk, sun-dried, and seldom laundered. Gannon carried a walnut-handled pistol in the right front pocket of his chaps; now and then he shot a downed animal with it, or heated the barrel over a small fire so he could shoulder brand a horse meant for Guthrie's herd.

His spurs were bigger, sharper, than those worn by the men who rode the horses he broke. Gannon's spurs could rip hide and hair off a mean animal. There has to be a streak of innate cruelty in a man if he's to be a good bronc tamer.

Gannon's face was rather flat, as though it had been slightly stepped on. His eyes always seemed half closed, as if he were thinking always about something secretive and

3

important. His face had a pleasant, rough-hewn quality about it, and there were scars here and there, from being pitched off onto rough ground, or having branches slap him in the face, or left by an angry man's fist. It was not an unpleasant face if you liked a man a little solemn and quiet in expression.

'One of these days I'm going somewhere,' Ben Clayton said earnestly. 'Next year, huh, when we're laid off?'

'You said that last year,' Gannon reminded him. He looked at Ben Clayton, his manner undisturbed by the young man's talk. 'You're always saying you're going somewhere. All right, let's go have a drink.' He started to turn but Ben put out his hand and touched Gannon on the arm.

'Do I look older, Charlie?' He grinned. 'Whiskey Pete had better just set the bottle down and make no remarks.'

'It's his joke,' Gannon said softly. 'Just a joke, Ben.'

'I'm tired of the joke,' Clayton said flatly. 'I asked you, do I look older?'

'Just one year older,' Gannon said. 'Now let's have that drink and get a head start on a long spell of loafing.'

It was a little early for a real good crowd to be lining the bar, but with Guthrie's laid-off hands in town Gannon and Clayton had to edge themselves out a place to get served.

The bartender came up and smiled; he was a

fat man who got that way drinking his own beer. 'Well, Charlie, Ben, good to see you gents again. Been a long summer.'

'Be a longer winter,' Gannon said. 'I expect you still buy that cheap whiskey.'

Pete smiled. 'I buy what my customers can afford.'

'How true that is,' Gannon said. 'Two here, and no complaints from this side of the bar.'

Pete put the glasses on the bar, but held one back a little. There was the hint of humor in his watery eyes when he glanced at Ben Clayton.

'Now don't start that again,' Clayton advised.

'Who, me? Start what?' Pete pretended surprise. 'I was just about to ask Charlie if he'd vouch for your age; you look a bit young.'

'That does it,' Ben Clayton said. He planted his hands firmly against the edge of the bar, gave himself a boost, and went over like an athlete taking the high jump. The bartender started to back away in sudden alarm, and Ben's boots caught him flush in the chest, driving him against the back counter. Glasses and bottles came down with a fracturing crash, and Ben kicked some of the debris aside with a sweep of his foot.

'Hey, Ben!' Gannon said, and young Clayton looked around.

Gannon's rock-hard fist caught him on the jaw and dropped him from view behind the bar. One of the cowboys standing down the bar

5

sighed and said, 'Just when it was gettin' good, too.'

'He's been building up to trouble,' Gannon said and walked around the end of the bar. He picked up a pan of water Pete kept there to rinse glasses in, and threw it on Ben Clayton, bringing him to a sputtering consciousness.

Pete approached with some suspicion; he rubbed his chest and breathed noisily. 'I've had enough, damn it. Every year it's the same thing, and I've had enough. I don't get forty dollars a year out of both of you, and it ain't worth it to me.' He looked at the broken glass. 'That's going to cost you ten dollars this time. I've had enough.'

'Ain't we all,' Gannon said and pulled Ben to his feet.

The young man rubbed his swelling jaw and said, 'Hell, you could have let me go a little longer, couldn't you?'

'You owe Whiskey Pete ten dollars,' Gannon said.

'For that?' He looked at the damage, snorted, then paid up.

The batwing doors swung open and fluttered to a close. Old Man Guthrie stomped in as though he had forgotten how to walk softly. He was seventy, weathered, cranky, and to hear him tell it, he'd been born old. A glance was enough to tell him what had happened. He said, 'Got a quick start this year, huh, Ben?' He wiggled his finger at Pete. 'Just set the bottle on the bar; I'll stand the first round.'

'I ought to call the marshal,' Whiskey Pete complained.

'You ought to learn when a joke's finished,' Guthrie said. 'Drink up, gents.' He looked at Clayton. 'You've had one, I assume.'

'No, I ain't,' Clayton said.

'Always drink first, then fight,' Guthrie advised. 'Then if you get thrown out, you've got something besides a bruised butt.'

'Well, I've had enough,' Whiskey Pete said. 'You two can take your piddlin' business elsewhere.'

Guthrie gave him a thunderstorm frown. 'Where the hell's your sense, Pete? After a man's seen nothing but wild country, mean horses, and Charlie Gannon for three months, he's got a thorn in him. If Lordsburg is too rough for you, go open a tea room in Kansas City.'

'Aaaahhh,' Pete said and began to sweep up the wreckage.

Gannon and Clayton had their first drink at the bar, on Guthrie, then took full glasses to a table and sat down away from the others. They were this way in most things, doing together, satisfied with their own company. Gannon drank some of his whiskey and felt it warm him; it hit a man solidly, especially when he hadn't had a drink for five months.

Ben Clayton said, 'This is a hell of a life.'

Gannon glanced sharply at him. 'What's wrong with it?'

'We're not getting anyplace, that's what's wrong with it.' He tossed off his drink and pushed the glass aside. 'Every fall we get paid off and we hang around town and do odd jobs just to keep going, and in the spring, when we're down to our last nickel, Guthrie hires us again.'

'So that's bad?'

'It's bad,' Ben Clayton said. 'I'm twenty-one and I've got my pay, and that's all.'

'What more do you want?'

Clayton shrugged. 'Just more, that's all.' He studied Charlie Gannon thoughtfully. 'It's all right for you to go drifting along. I never did understand that, Charlie. How can a man be so damned satisfied with nothing.' He reached across the table and took Gannon by the arm, speaking more softly. 'How many horses did we catch and break for Guthrie this year?'

'A hundred, I guess. Maybe a few more.'

'Yeah, I figure a hundred myself. In dollars, how much do you reckon they'd be worth?'

'Five thousand,' Gannon said, frowning. 'What's the point?'

Ben Clayton took his money from his pocket and laid it on the table. 'A hundred and forty dollars, Charlie, after paying ten to Pete. You get a hundred and eighty. But put it together and it's a long way from five thousand.'

'Well, I was figuring that five thousand as top price,' Gannon said. 'More than likely we'd only clear three or a little better.'

'It's still a long way from what we've got,' Clayton insisted.

'Yeah, it is. But Guthrie's got an investment. Don't forget that.'

'We've got an investment too,' Ben said, patting the money. 'Right here.'

Charlie Gannon leaned back in his chair, and, with deliberation, built a cigaret before speaking. 'Ben, what goose chase are you trying to lead me on?' He lit his smoke, then sat there, sprawled in the chair as though he had been looking forward to this moment of leisure for a long time. 'Ben, why don't you relax and take life easy? I swear, you're the hoppinest man I've ever seen. Up before it's light, then talkin' instead of sleepin'. Ben, this summer you've tried to get me to quit horse wranglin' and get a job as an Indian agent, get a job scoutin' for the army in Arizona, buy cattle in Mexico and sell 'em here, start a small spread of my own, get a wife and get married, and take a job as marshal to Wyatt Earp over in Tombstone. Now what is it?'

'If you're going to take that attitude, I ain't going to say,' Clayton said stubbornly. 'Charlie, I wanted all those things for your good.'

'For me?' He laughed. 'What the hell do I need, Ben? I mean, that I don't already have?'

Ben Clayton hesitated, as though he was being forced to say things he didn't want to say. 'Charlie, how many years have you been stomping broncs?'

9

'Nine, ten, I guess.'

'How long can you keep it up?' He held up his hand when Gannon opened his mouth to speak. 'You've had your legs busted, and your arms, and you know as well as I do that it's been hell to get out of the blankets some mornings. You need something different, Charlie. I've really been thinking on this.'

'It seems that you have,' Gannon said softly.

Clayton studied him, his young face gravely concerned. 'You're not sore at me, are you, for talking out that way?'

'No,' Gannon said. 'Why should I be, Ben? Hell, any man in town can notice my new limp, the one I didn't have last year. I figure I've got four or five more years, Ben. Until I'm forty anyway.'

'Then what?'

Charlie Gannon shrugged his shoulders and finished his drink. 'Who looks that far ahead, Ben?'

'I do,' Clayton said. 'Will you listen to me?'

'Sure, don't I always? But you're young and full of talk, Ben.'

'This time it's more than talk,' Ben Clayton said. 'Dog gone, it's kind of funny. When we first met, it was you that looked after me, but now I feel as though I got to look after you.'

'Hell, I ain't that old,' Gannon said firmly. 'Your jaw hurt? You're going to have a hell of a bruise.'

'It's all right,' Clayton said. He hunched his

10

shoulders and leaned as far as he could toward Gannon. 'It fair to itches me to catch and break horses for Guthrie, and he paying us what he does.'

'The going wage,' Gannon reminded him.

'Let's strike out for ourselves, Charlie. We got until spring.' He reached over and fished the sack of tobacco from Gannon's pocket and made a smoke. 'I hear that there's lots of horses running wild in Utah. A man could winter out up there, and come back with a good pile, if he played his cards right.'

Gannon smiled. 'Yeah, if the Piutes didn't lift his hair, or the winter didn't kill him, or some other horse hunter didn't shoot him for foolin' around his territory.' He shook his head. 'Sounds good, Ben; I've got to admit that, but the two of us couldn't swing it.'

'Why couldn't we?' He was full of enthusiasm, easily carried away by it. 'We got a little over three hundred dollars between us, Charlie. That's enough to put an outfit together. I've got two horses and you've got three. I've got it all figured out.'

'It sure seems that you have,' Gannon said. 'How many horses do you expect to break come spring?'

'Not saddle broke, Charlie. Just slicker broke, enough to drive 'em back. Oh, we may break three or four for our own use, the best of the lot, but the others we'll sell as is.' He drew deeply on the cigaret, then ground it out

11

beneath his boot. 'It's bust or not for me, Charlie. I just can't stand to think of another winter hanging around town.'

'It figures,' Gannon remarked. 'At twenty-one, a man's just bustin' his breeches.' He frowned briefly. 'Ben, I'd have to think on it.'

'Don't think too long,' Clayton said seriously. 'Charlie, I've made up *my* mind. Tomorrow morning I'm going to start putting together my outfit.'

'You'd go it alone?'

'If I have to,' Clayton said.

'Ben, you couldn't do it alone. Indians would get you, or a bad horse. You're talking like a fool now.'

'You're getting that tone, Charlie,' Clayton said, a mild warning in his voice. 'You coming with me or not?'

Gannon frowned slightly. 'Do you have to push me?'

'You could stand a push, Charlie.'

'I like the way I am,' Gannon said and slowly got up. 'I'll see you later.'

'Sure,' Ben Clayton said. 'Charlie, you remember something, huh?'

'What?'

'You need me. You won't last four more years without me.' A hard, prideful resentment came into Gannon's eyes, but it didn't stop Ben Clayton. 'I pulled you out of three tight ones this year, and you know it. You've been busted so many times that you ache all over, and it's

12

slowing you down, Charlie. I'm young. I make up the difference. You think about that.'

Charlie Gannon looked at him for a long moment, then said, 'Ben, I always had the notion that I was taking care of you. I taught you all you know about horses, and I guess I've pulled you out of a few tight ones too. So I guess we're even there. But don't lead me around by the hand, Ben. I just don't like it at all.' A note of sadness came into his voice. 'I'm getting slow all right. Getting tired, Ben, but up to a minute ago, I wasn't much ashamed of it. I just wish you hadn't said those things.'

He turned then and walked out of the saloon, limping a little, and on the porch he stopped to roll another smoke. It would give him time to think, to calm himself a little. A full darkness was settling fast; lamps came on along the street, and the after-supper crowd began to show itself.

Gannon turned down the street and walked along until he came to a building sporting fan lights over the wide door. An overhead sign advertised Madam Fontaine's Terpsichorean Palace: Six Beautiful Girls: Free Lunch at the Bar.

He went in and found only the helper spreading soap chips on the floor; the musicians were not on the small bandstand, and Gannon walked toward the hallway in back, pausing at a partially closed door. He heard a woman laugh, then someone picked up

13

a deck of cards and shuffled them.

Gannon knocked.

'Come in.'

He pushed the door all the way open and Mildred Jennings smiled. A man sat across from her; he nodded to Gannon and said, 'Want to learn all my secrets, Charlie?'

'I'd never use 'em,' Gannon said. He toed a chair around and sat down. His glance touched Harry Graves. 'There's a lot of Guthrie's money rattling around in pockets over at the saloon.' He smiled at the gambler. 'How big a per cent do you figure to get, Harry?'

'Oh, a little more than a quarter of it, I'd say.' He arched an eyebrow. 'Would you care to contribute?'

'I don't understand card games,' Gannon admitted. 'And I can't keep from yellin' when I've got a good hand, or frownin' when it's poor. I always lose.'

Mildred Jennings got up to put the coffee pot on the small stove. She was tall and slender and Gannon didn't think she was a very good dancer, but she was pretty, which was more appreciated in Lordsburg than studied grace. She came back and sat down, looking first at Harry Graves, then at Gannon.

'Why all the smiles?' she asked jokingly. 'You look like you'd just come from a funeral.'

'That fool kid's got notions again,' Gannon said. 'Wants to winter out in the wild-horse country.'

14

'I guess there's nothing wrong with that,' Graves said, 'if you like sleeping with wild horses.' He was a small, delicate-handed man who never could quite take anything seriously. 'Most men are glad to stay out of Piute country, Charlie.'

'That's what I said, more or less,' Gannon admitted. He blew out a long breath. 'One of these days I'm going to give him a good kick in the butt and boot him out on his own. We'll see how he likes that.'

There was an edge of seriousness to his voice and Mildred Jennings was alarmed by it. 'I wouldn't do that, Charlie. You'd be sorry afterward.'

'I guess I would,' he said, rising. 'Can I see you later, Mildred?'

'Yes, around midnight,' she said. 'Won't you stay and have some coffee?'

He shook his head. 'Guess I'll walk around a little. I feel restless.'

After he went out, Harry Graves picked up the cards, made a fan of them, a ladder shuffle, then dealt himself a pat hand. She got the coffee and poured, then sat down, and Graves said, 'What did you tell him that for?'

'Tell him what?'

'About not breaking off with Ben. Clayton needs Charlie like a hole in the seat of his pants.'

She showed him a sudden and firm anger. 'You fool, Harry. If he loses Ben, he loses

15

everything.' She put a spoon of sugar in her coffee and sat there stirring it, her dark eyes veiled by long lashes. 'I've often wondered why Charlie took to Ben in the beginning; he was always a man who liked being alone. Maybe it was because he suspected then that there wasn't much left. He's proud, Harry. And it must have frightened him to know deep down that the steam was gone. He used to be able to sit on anything with hair, but not now. Any good saddle horse working off ginger on a cold morning can throw him.' She forgot about the coffee and sat there with her hands folded in her lap. 'He knows Ben's been carrying the heavy end of the load, but he's taught Ben and in that way has paid it off. But it must be a hard thing now, because Ben knows as much about his work as Charlie does, and there's no way to square it any more.'

'Hell,' Graves said, slightly disgusted, 'you'll be crying for him next.'

'Oh, shut your cynical mouth!' Mildred snapped. 'I like Charlie Gannon. A squarer man never walked on this earth. That's hard for you to believe, isn't it?'

'No, I believe it,' Harry Graves said. He neatly decked the cards and put them into a tooled leather case which fit his inside coat pocket. 'Mildred, why the hell don't you marry him?' He looked at her a moment, waiting for her answer. And when he got none he said, 'No, I suppose you already know it wouldn't

16

work. What you have would not replace Ben Clayton's crutch.'

She glared at him, then said bitterly, 'Why don't you go over to the saloon and trim the suckers?'

'It's a noble thought,' he admitted, rising. Then he smiled and touched her shoulder. 'The biggest favor you could do Charlie would be to make him face the truth. Couldn't you do that for him?'

'No, I couldn't,' she said.

Harry Graves shrugged. 'Well, it's not my business.'

'That's exactly right; it's not your business.'

He turned to the door and paused there. 'You're full of the milk of human kindness, so do Charlie one more favor. Talk him into going along with Ben. I wouldn't want to see him turn into Lordsburg's town bum.'

He went out before she could throw something at him, then the impulse to do just that died in her and she sat there, disturbed by the talk.

CHAPTER TWO

Ben Clayton sat in the lobby of the hotel at one of the small writing desks, a paper before him and the stub of a pencil in his mouth, as he thought about the list he was making up. He

17

glanced at Charlie Gannon when he came over, pulling a chair around so he could sit down.

'Got your hair cut, I see,' Ben said. 'New shirt, too.'

'From the skin out,' Gannon said. About him were the strong odors of soap and toilet water, and he kept lifting his hand to the back of his neck as though terribly conscious of the barbered bareness of it. He no longer wore his chaps, brush jacket and spurs; they were in the stable with his saddle and horse. 'What you makin' out there, Ben?' He asked it casually, as if he didn't already know.

'List of what we're going to need,' Ben Clayton said.

Gannon sighed. 'This is more'n a notion, huh?'

'I'm dead serious and you know it,' Clayton told him.

'Let's see your list,' Gannon said, his manner patronizing. Clayton handed it over and Gannon made a grand business of studying it. Now and then he asked a question. 'You've got a buckboard down here.'

'Britt, at the stable, said he'd sell it for thirty-five dollars.'

'And the team?'

'My horses can be broken to harness,' Clayton said. 'And with the three you've got—'

'I see,' Gannon said, and read on. He had to admit that Clayton hadn't left out anything. A

18

horse hunter needed certain tools, and Clayton had them all down there: pick, shovels, two rolls of heavy wire, nails, blankets, two hatchets and an ax, and four hundred feet of rope. The rest was mostly food and camping stuff. Gannon handed it back. 'If I went along, the two of us still would need help. Five men anyway, Ben.'

'We can get by,' Clayton insisted stubbornly. 'We'll have to pass up the big herds, Charlie, but we'll get by.' He clasped his hands together and regarded Gannon seriously. 'I don't want you to think I don't appreciate all you taught me, but I want you to come with me. I can really use you, Charlie.'

Gannon stared for a moment, then laughed. '*You* can use ME? Ben, I've forgot more about horse wranglin' than you'll ever know.' He laughed again as though this was the best joke he'd ever heard. 'For two cents I'd go along just to see you bust yourself proper.'

Ben Clayton didn't say anything; he just took two pennies out of his shirt pocket and laid them on the desk.

Gannon glanced at them and pursed his full lips. 'Calling me, huh?'

'Yep.'

'There's going to be one boss,' he said. 'Me.'

'I'll buy it,' Clayton said seriously. 'You're the boss, Charlie. Only we got to agree now that there's one decision you can't make.'

'And that is?'

19

'That we won't give up before spring; we stay out the winter, snow, Indians, and all.'

'It won't take that long to whip you down to pint size,' Charlie Gannon said.

'Nevertheless, that's part of the deal.'

'You've sold it,' Gannon said. He took his money from his pocket and tossed it on the table. 'Make a pile,' he invited.

Ben Clayton grinned and tossed his on it; they shook hands solemnly.

Once Gannon decided a thing, he did it; that was his way, never to wait until later, never to let any excuse put a thing off. With the list in hand, he and Clayton spent the evening buying. As the boss he handled the money, did all the haggling, made the final decisions. There was extra bedding to buy, and ground sheets, for they might lose one or two outfits before spring. Accidents happened even to careful men who knew what they were doing. They bought two small tents and one fairly large one. After some trading they parted with both six-shooters and, with a little to boot, bought two .44-40 rifles, a .22 single shot for small game, and a double-barreled shotgun. Gannon hated to pay a dollar thirty-five a box for .44 shells but he really thought they ought to have two hundred rounds of rifle ammunition, along with a box of twenty-twos, and a dozen shotgun shells; they came twenty in a wooden box, double 00 buck, and he settled for that.

By the time closing hour forced them out of the store, they'd bought everything they needed—food, bedding, cooking ware. All sat on the back porch to be loaded in the morning.

They had thirty-four dollars left and split it between them before going to the saloon for a drink. It was one of the liveliest spots in town now. The piano player thumped out a racy tune, and a babble of voices filled the room. Cigar smoke clung to the ceiling beams like a rank fog and the hanging lanterns, trying to cut through it, highlighted the density of it. At his table, Harry Graves sat like a wax image, only his hands moving as he dealt cards. Now and then he spoke, to call or to raise or to ask, 'Cards?'

Clayton and Gannon took their drinks and stood near the bar, out of the customers' way. Clayton watched Harry Graves at his work, then said, 'I feel like bucking the tiger.'

'It's your seventeen dollars,' Gannon said dryly.

Clayton looked at him and smiled. 'Didn't you ever feel lucky, Charlie?'

'No,' Gannon said.

'Well, I feel lucky,' he said. 'Come on.'

They walked over to the table and Graves glanced at them briefly, just enough to say hello with a lift of the eyebrow; he never really took his attention off the game.

No one was playing for very high stakes and Gannon thought that after a night at the table

21

Graves might make a sum total of thirty dollars. Multiply that three or four times and you had a fair idea of what he earned in a month.

Ben Clayton said, 'Harry, let's play a new game.'

He spoke during a lull, when Graves was shuffling cards. The gambler looked at him, then said, 'What kind of game?'

'High card,' Clayton said. He grinned and seemed very young, very innocent. 'I don't have the time to lose my money slow.' He pointed to the cards. 'Pick out someone to shuffle. Then put the deck on the table. I draw one off the top. So do you. High card takes the money.'

'You do want to lose quick,' Graves said. 'All right.' He glanced at the men sitting there, then raised his eyes to Charlie Gannon. A smile raised the ends of Graves' mustache. 'It's not that I think you're any more honest than the next guy, Charlie, but just that you're not quick enough with your hands to manipulate a deck of cards. You shuffle. Bet your money, Ben.'

'Five dollars,' Clayton said, laying the bill on the table.

Gannon shuffled and placed the cards face down. Clayton took one, then Graves, who turned his face up. 'Ten of diamonds,' he said.

Ben Clayton had the three of hearts. As Graves took his money, he said, 'Ten dollars.'

And took a card. He didn't wait for Graves, just flipped it over, showing a Queen of spades. Graves drew a five of clubs and paid up.

'Twenty dollars,' Ben Clayton said. He won again, and Graves wanted the deck reshuffled.

While Gannon was doing it, he said, 'You really want to win it all or lose it all, don't you, Ben?'

'That's the idea of the game, isn't it?' Gannon put the cards on the table, and Clayton said, 'Forty dollars.' He took his card and turned it up, a three of hearts.

Graves laughed heartily and drew, then let his humor fade when he showed a two of spades. 'God damn it,' he said, and chewed on his cigar.

Ben Clayton took seventy dollars and folded it before putting it in his shirt pocket. He bet ten dollars, which brought an immense frown to Harry Graves' forehead.

'Real smart,' Graves said, and waited for Clayton to draw his card. Clayton lost, and bet ten more. He lost again. Without dipping into his seventy dollar pocket, he produced two one dollar bills and laid them on the table.

Graves said, 'You're a real cheapskate, Ben.'

'Yep,' Clayton said, and turned over an ace of hearts.

He doubled his bet, won, doubled again, and won again. He left the sixteen dollars laying there and asked Charlie Gannon to shuffle the cards.

This play was drawing some attention now; men brought their drinks from the bar and ringed the table. Harry Graves kept chewing the end of his cigar, and tried not to look irritated.

Clayton drew a four of clubs, which beat Graves' deuce of spades.

He swore softly when Clayton picked up twenty dollars of the money and left sixteen. Harry Graves looked at the money a moment, then said, 'I've had enough of this stupidity!'

A groan went up from the onlookers, and Ben Clayton smiled. 'Not steep enough for you, Harry?'

'You're putting all of *my* money in your pocket,' Graves said flatly. 'You ride your winning streak, then jump off so I can't win any of it back.'

'It could work the other way around,' Charlie Gannon pointed out.

Ben Clayton took the money from his pocket, put ten with it to make an even hundred, and laid it on the table. He drew a card without hesitation and turned up a six of hearts. It wasn't a very good card, and everyone knew it. Graves hesitated, then drew his, a deuce.

His anger was an explosive curse in his throat and he reared up out of his chair, sweeping the cards to the floor. He glared at Ben Clayton, but surprisingly turned his anger on Charlie Gannon. 'I thought you shuffled

24

those cards!'

'You saw me,' Gannon said evenly. 'Give him another chance, Ben.'

'I'd as soon quit,' Clayton said. 'We've got three pack horses here, Charlie. And enough to load 'em.'

Gannon was still looking at Graves. 'Make it six,' he said. 'We'll even let Harry shuffle his own deck.'

A flicker of surprise came into Graves' eyes, and vanished. Still pretending anger, he sat down, paid out all the money he had in his wallet and shuffled the cards while Gannon watched him closely.

'Now cut 'em,' Gannon said. 'Two piles. Ben, you draw from one pile. Harry from the other.' He switched his glance to Ben Clayton. 'You first.'

Ben Clayton hesitated, then turned up a king. A grin spread across his untroubled face, and he laughed softly at the thought of having four hundred dollars. But his laughter died when Charlie Gannon reached out, pulled a man's pistol from his holster, and cocked it.

'Now you draw your card, Harry, and if it's an ace, I'm going to blow your head off.'

'What?' Graves said. He looked at the gun, then at Gannon's eyes, and swallowed hard. 'I'll swear out a warrant against you for this, Charlie.'

'Only if I'm wrong and there isn't an ace there,' Gannon said softly. 'But I'm willing to

25

bet it's there, and that you know it's there. Prove me wrong, Harry.'

For a moment Graves sat perfectly still, then he sighed and shook his head. He pushed against the table with his hands and went to the bar for a drink.

One of the men said, 'Pick up the money, son. You won it.'

'Not until I see his card,' Ben Clayton said. He reached out and flipped over the ace of diamonds. A murmur, a half-angry mutter rippled through the men standing around the table; they were remembering all the bets they had lost at Harry Graves' table, all the suspicions men have against professional gamblers, all the things they really knew and never had been able to prove.

And Graves at the bar, with his back turned, heard the tone and knew what it meant. He whirled and tried to draw his gun but some man plucked it from his fingers and they swarmed over him like ants devouring a scrap. He went to the floor beneath their weight, and when they pulled him erect, his coat was torn and there was a bloody streak on his cheek.

'Get a pole!' somebody shouted, and two men dashed out to tear off a hitch rail. They brought it into the saloon, and a piece of rope was produced from the back room. Eager, angry hands ripped and stripped away Graves' clothes until he was clad only in his long underwear. He kicked and fought and was

26

battered about a bit until he saw that it was no use.

They bound his feet together, slipped the pole between his legs and went out with him, giving him a cruel ride up and down the street. Gannon and Ben Clayton took no part in this, but they went outside to stand on the porch and watch. It was a regular parade, and at first the city marshal was going to put a stop to it until he found out what it was all about, then he crossed over to the saloon porch and stood near Clayton and Gannon.

Graves was dunked two or three times in the watering trough, and he clung to the pole like a bear, trying to ease the jolt as the men dashed about with it.

'He's had enough,' Gannon said at last.

The marshal glanced at him, then said, 'It's better than getting shot.'

There was no argument in Gannon. He said, 'Are you going to stop it or do I have to?'

'All right, I'll stop it,' the marshal said, and stepped down to meet them. They were coming back to the saloon. He waved his arms to indicate that it was all over, and they set the pole down. Graves could not stand and two men obligingly pulled the pole from between his bound legs. 'Now you fellas put that back where you found it,' the marshal said. 'Somebody might want to tie up their horses.'

There was laughter at this, but Gannon didn't smile. He looked at Harry Graves, and

27

the gambler was moving his head, his eyes, searching out Gannon. When he found him, Graves said, 'Charlie, I swear to you, I'll kill you for this.'

'Do you want to do it now?' Gannon asked, his manner calm.

'I'll pick a time,' Graves said.

'But not in this town,' the marshal said. He was a big, block-faced man who'd handled the tough ones, and the drunk ones, and more than a few crooked ones. 'Be out of Lordsburg by morning, Harry. I'm giving you more than you deserve.'

The crowd lost interest now; there was no immediate promise of trouble. They went back into the saloon to have another drink and talk it over. It was an exciting night.

Graves got to his hands and knees and stayed there a few minutes; the ride on the pole had all but crippled him. Without looking at Ben or Charlie he said, 'If either of you try to help me, I'll kill you.'

'He's got killing on his mind,' Ben Clayton said, sounding sad.

'That's a fact,' Gannon said. He looked closely at Clayton. 'What did you want to do, take his money and end up friends?' He laughed briefly. 'Ben, you've got a thing or two to learn about gamblers.' He walked over to where Harry Graves was trying to get up. 'Are you hurt bad?'

'What the hell do you care?' Graves asked.

28

He made a waving motion with his hand to keep Gannon away, and the man turned back to Ben Clayton.

'Let's put up in the stable,' Clayton said and they went on down the street. They walked a way in silence, then Ben said, 'You know, we ought to load the buckboard tonight. I wouldn't want anyone to steal that stuff on the back porch.'

Gannon's grunt was his sign of agreement, and they hitched up the two saddle horses, after some fuss, and drove through the dark alley. While they wrestled boxes and bundles, Clayton kept turning over in his mind Harry Graves' threat.

Finally he said, 'Let's have a smoke.' While they rolled cigarets, Clayton went on with his talk. 'It bothers me, what Harry said about killin' us.'

'Go back and give him his money and he'll forget all about it,' Charlie Gannon told him.

'You're jokin'?'

'Naw, I'm serious. Did you ever look in a gambler's eyes when he was on a winnin' streak? The money shines there, Ben. You had it tonight.'

Clayton laughed self-consciously. 'Well, hell, that's the first money I ever got in my life that I didn't have to work for.'

'What do you mean, you didn't work for? If Harry finds the right time, you may have to work like the devil for it.' He sat down and put

29

his back against the building. 'I'm kind of sorry I bought into that game the way I did.'

'Why did you? I can handle myself.'

Gannon thought a moment, then said, 'I guess I thought about how long the summer's been, and how small the pay was, and just couldn't stand to see you lose it. He was going to turn up an ace, Ben.'

'It beats me how; I watched the deal.' He hunkered down, comfortable in the darkness. Only his cigaret end glowed when he drew on it, casting a brief, reddish glow on his face. 'Did you see him make a split, Charlie?'

'I didn't see a thing,' Gannon admitted.

Ben Clayton blew out a long breath and tacked a laugh on the end of it. 'Seems that you was takin' a bigger gamble than he was. Which is odd; you ain't much for that kind of thing.'

'I have been,' Gannon said, rising. 'You keep forgetting I've got some years on you, and a lot passed before you came along.'

They took the heavily loaded buckboard back to the stable and unhitched the team. While they were putting the horses in the stalls, the marshal came around.

He said, 'I just came from Madam Fontaine's place. Mildred wants to see you.'

Gannon knew a moment of guilty conscience. He had forgotten to go back. The marshal stood around, as though he meant to walk part way with Gannon; they left together

30

and walked a ways before the marshal spoke.

'I'm glad you showed Graves up tonight, because I always had a hunch he wasn't honest.'

Gannon abruptly stopped and looked at the marshal. 'Why the hell is it people always say that? Harry was no crook.' He waved his stubby hands. 'Sure, he cut a thin deck tonight because he was mad at the way Ben pushed him around, and a little worried about Ben quitting the game. It's a risk every gambler runs, a player leaving when the bulk of the money is in his pocket.'

'But you called him and made it stick.'

'Yeah,' Gannon said wearily. 'And now I wish I hadn't. I made an enemy for four hundred dollars. Too bad a man can't make friends for that.'

The marshal took off his flat-crowned hat and ran his fingers through his hair. 'Damned if I understand you, Charlie. I don't know what you're for or against.'

'Half the time I don't know myself,' Gannon admitted and walked off alone. He entered Madam Fontaine's place by the side door and one of the floor men saw him and called Mildred from the wings. She gave him a wan smile to let him know she wasn't too put out, then nodded and led the way back to the guest parlor. She fixed him a drink, then sat down and looked at him solemnly.

'Charlie, I feel like cussing you good for

what you did to Harry tonight.'

'Why don't you? For what I did I've got a cussing coming.'

She seemed surprised to hear him say that; her expression showed it. 'I don't understand. Are you sorry?'

'Yes. I did it for Ben and he didn't even have sense enough to see it.' He rolled a smoke and lit it. 'Well, we're going to clear out in the morning. I've got to keep the kid alive until he gets some sense.' His grin was lop-sided. 'Be spring before I see you again, Mildred.'

'Well, spring into fall, fall into spring. What difference does it make? Me, I'm not going anyplace. I don't think you are either. But you take care of yourself, you hear, Charlie?'

He looked at her, puzzled. 'Nothing will happen to me. What do you worry about me for, Mildred? Do I mean that much to you?'

'If you mean, do I have an eye on you for a husband, the answer is no.' She folded and unfolded her hands. 'Did you ever do anything but horse wrangling?'

'Nope,' he said. 'Got started as a kid and never saw fit to change.'

'And what'll you do when you're—well, too old to take it?'

He shook his head. 'I'm thirty-six, Mildred. Don't put me on crutches yet.' But he knew what she meant and had no answer for her. 'I'll find something. The horse is here to stay.' He swirled what remained of his whiskey around

32

in the glass, and drank it and sat there, rotating the glass between his rough palms. 'I'd never let on to Ben about this, Mildred, but it scares me at times, when I get to thinking about it. The trouble is, I don't know what I can do because I've never done anything but wrangling. When I was younger, I'd always tell myself that I'd cut out from the herd one of these days and try railroading, or mining, or herdin' sheep up in Montana. Bein' a farmer's crossed my mind, but I never cut out, never tried any of those things. I'm a wrangler because I know that and I can cut it all right. After a while a man gets scared of what he can't do, and the older he gets, the more he needs to know, and the more scared he gets that he'll find out he can't do anything.'

She regarded him seriously for a moment. 'Why can't you tell Ben?'

'Because he'd laugh,' Gannon said. 'Hell, I'd have laughed too, if a man had told me that when I was Ben's age. The world's full of hills to look over when you're twenty-one, Mildred. It's just plain fun to run down 'em. Kind of funny, though, as each year's passed I've looked more and more to this winter lay-off, and Ben's liked it less and less. For me, it's a time to get the kinks out of my back and get over all the limps and bumps the summer fetched me. Those things just bounce off Ben, though, like he was one of those new rubber boots the Easterners wear.'

'I'm glad you're going with Ben,' Mildred said. 'Not because it's Indian country or anything like that. He just needs you, Charlie.'

He looked at her and smiled and shook his head. 'You didn't have to say that to me. Tonight, Ben put it pretty straight to me that he's been packing more than his share of the load. No, I need him now. He wants me along because we've been partners for five years, and the habit's still with him, the two of us being together. But it's going to wear off, Mildred. And Ben'll go his way and be real embarrassed about saying good-bye.'

Her face was grave and still and regret was in her eyes. 'I'm sorry you know that, Charlie. Believe me, I am.'

'Yeah,' he said. 'Me too.'

CHAPTER THREE

They drove north by east with their buckboard and horses, into the Apache country where it was all mountains and sky and lonesome miles that were longer than any miles they'd ever traveled before. They took directions by the sun and a small pocket compass, for there were no horizons, just ragged ridges and sandy canyon floors and trails undefined and unfriendly. It was a country where a man rode with his head constantly turning, and his rifle in his hands, the finger on the trigger.

Their first stop, after eight days of travel, was Fort Apache. They watered up there, talked to the civilian scout about the Indian activity, and after learning that the Mimbrenos were 'busy' that fall, they pushed on.

For a time they were in an arid, desert-like land, where the only trees to be found were along the banks of infrequent streams, and then only scrub oak and juniper and stunted cottonwoods grew. The rest was cactus, Spanish bayonet and palo verdes and massive biznagas.

At night camp they never made a fire, and one slept while the other stood guard, for there were Apaches about. But they never saw them. Not once during the sixteen-day march to Fort Defiance.

The army was surprised to see two civilians traveling alone, more surprised that they had traveled so far without unpleasantness. The post adjutant was a graying captain; he insisted they be his guests while the horses rested, and since this made good sense, they thanked him and enjoyed a bath in his personal tub.

That evening they had supper in his quarters, a rather plain adobe 'apartment' connected to a long row of apartments. His name was Anders and this was his third tour on the Arizona frontier. He was a dry-humored man of considerable knowledge and ability.

35

'It's always been my theory,' Anders said, 'that any man, alert and well armed, could pass through Apache country with little or no difficulty. Of course, I've never before suggested that anyone attempt to prove this, but I would say that you gentlemen have.'

'What kind of a trail goes north into Utah, Captain?' Gannon asked.

'I'm afraid there isn't much of any trail,' Anders said, smiling. 'A man just picks his way the best he can. Rough country. There's some hellish big canyons with cliff dwellings dug into the rock faces. Some prehistoric aborigines, I'd say. Stay clear of those. A man could lose himself in there and spend forty years getting out.' He got up from the table and went to his writing desk to bring back a map. After spreading it out, he said, 'I'd go due north of here, eight or ten days, into the horse country. You'll know it because it opens up into desert and huge, flat-topped mesas.' He looked from one to the other as though he had just thought of something. 'Are you after horses, gentlemen?'

'That's right,' Clayton said. 'That's horse country.'

Captain Anders shook his head and folded the map; he gave it to Charlie Gannon before speaking. 'Yes, and it's Piute country, also. And about horsed out, too. Joe Kerry and his bunch work that country. They've got some deal with the Indians. No one else has gone in

36

there and come out with his hair.' He scrubbed a heavy hand across his mouth. 'You might work west, five or six day's travel. Fine wild horse country in there. Trouble is, it's thick with Piutes, and a few scattered Mormon families.'

'Don't the Indians bother 'em?' Clayton asked, surprised.

'Oh, now and then some buck will get drunk and kill one of them, but the Mormons seem to get along with everyone.' He smiled. 'It's real horse country, and no one's worked it that I know of. Joe Kerry tried last year and got his ears pinned back. He lost three men and a lot of equipment. Of course he talks about going back, but I don't think he will. Catching horses is hard enough work without keeping an eye out for Indians at the same time.' He offered them cigars from a tin cannister, and Gannon took one, but Ben Clayton preferred to roll a cigaret. 'Kerry's on the post now if you want to talk to him.'

Charlie Gannon thought about this for a minute, then shook his head. 'There's nothing I want to ask him.' He accepted the light Anders offered, and thanked him with the lift of his eyebrows. 'As I see it, no good would come of me telling Kerry where we're going since he's already been there.'

'And just because he got run out is no sign we will,' Clayton said with youthful optimism.

'You have a point there,' Anders agreed.

'Gentlemen, I'm sorry my quarters are so small I can't offer you decent beds.'

'That's all right, Captain,' Gannon said. 'We planned to bunk in the stable near our goods.' He got up and Clayton followed suit.

Anders went to the door with them and shook hands all around. 'Breakfast is at six at the officers' mess. I'd be delighted to share my table.'

'Thanks,' Gannon said. 'We'll be there.'

As they walked across the dark parade to the stable compound, Ben Clayton said, 'He sure was nice, huh, Charlie?'

'What did he have to gain by being any other way?'

'Well, I don't know. But I just meant, he didn't have to be so accommodating.'

Their horses were inside the stable, in stalls, but the buckboard, sagging under its load, was parked outside by the door. As they approached they saw two men standing by the wagon, and a third came out of the stable with a lantern; all three started to examine the loaded buckboard.

Gannon and Clayton increased their pace and came up suddenly. The three men turned, annoyed at the interruption. The one who held the lantern was a dark-complexioned man, quite tall, and pole-slender.

In the bland flood of lantern light, he offered them a smile. They could only see the lower part of his face, for the tin smoke-chimney cut off the light and cast most of it outward and downward.

'I guess this is your rig,' he said.

'And I guess you've got no business snooping around it,' Gannon said flatly. 'Who the hell are you anyway?'

'Joe Kerry.' He held the lantern a little higher, a little closer to Ben Clayton.

'Take that thing out of my eyes,' Clayton said calmly.

'Just wanted to take a lo—'

Clayton swung his arm, caught the base of the lantern with his fist and knocked it out of Kerry's hand. It struck and came apart and spilled its fuel, but it went out instead of catching fire.

'Get the hell away from our goods,' Clayton said.

Joe Kerry laughed pleasantly. 'Now, sonny, don't get worked up. Every year I got to put up with a new batch of horse hunters. Didn't the army tell you this is my territory? I sell all my horses to the army, and they buy all the horses they need from me.' He spread his hands in an appeal for understanding, cooperation. 'And every one I tell the same thing to: don't go any farther north. There'll be trouble if you do.'

'Did anybody ever tell you to go to hell?' Gannon asked.

'Why, a few have,' Kerry said, still pleasant about it all. 'George here, and his brother, Al, had to bang a few heads together. And that's a

39

lot of trouble, so we just kept the outfits.' He looked from one to the other. 'That seems fair, don't it?'

Gannon was too staggered by the gall of this man to answer him. Ben Clayton recovered more quickly. He said, 'Charlie, which one do you want?'

'Hell, I don't care. You got a preference?'

'Naw, but since you're the boss, I thought you ought to—'

'Right!' Gannon said and suddenly sank his fist in Joe Kerry's stomach. Kerry hadn't been quite set for that, and the blow caught him with muscles relaxed. His breath exploded out of him, and he jackknifed like a snapped hinge. He struck the ground knees first and they plopped in the dust. Then the two brothers came to life, both jumping Ben Clayton.

George was big and heavy and bull-like, and his rush alone would have carried Ben to the ground had Ben not flexed at the hips and let George flop over him like a man performing an acrobatic dance.

It was a good start for Gannon and Ben Clayton, but only a start. With amazing power of recuperation Joe Kerry got off the ground and went after Gannon while Ben and Al pounded each other with fists. George was groping around, getting up, trying to decide who he should help; he couldn't seem to make up his mind who needed it most, his brother or Joe Kerry.

This hesitancy was enough to allow Ben Clayton to slam Al against the buckboard with a fractured jaw, and when the man wilted to the ground, George piled on Ben's back and bore him down.

The ruckus alerted the stable guard, who came on the run with lanterns. Gannon and Joe Kerry were locked in each other's grip, thrashing around on the ground, each trying to end up on top. Now and then they landed a blow, the impact solid, like a raw steak slapped on a butcher's block.

How Ben got out from under George, he never knew, but he came erect an instant ahead of the big man and caught him while he was still on one knee. The blow came up low, traveled fast, and stopped suddenly, an explosion against George's mouth. He fetched back, arms waving, and cracked his skull solidly against the axle nut. Then he fell forward on his face and lay still.

Ben Clayton was all for taking a breather, until he looked at Charlie Gannon, on the bottom, being pelted by Joe Kerry's fists. Without hesitation, Ben jumped into the air, swung his legs just right, and kicked Joe Kerry clean off Gannon. The man rolled over three times, a welter of blood on the side of his head, and he never knew what hit him. Gannon got up, feeling his tender face. Around them a dozen troopers stood, lanterns held high. Al was moaning and trying to sit up, but it didn't look as though he would make it.

The sergeant of the guard walked over and looked at Kerry, then at the other two. He said, 'I can't recall this ever happenin' before.'

'First time for everything,' Ben said, between sawn breaths. His nose was bloody and one lip was puffing badly, and there was a darkening spot on his cheekbone. He looked at Charlie Gannon, who was shaking his head, trying to still the ringing there. 'What was you doin' on the bottom, Charlie? Don't you know up from down?'

'Seems that I don't,' Gannon said. He groaned a little when he walked over to the watering trough, took off his shirt and splashed water on his face.

The sergeant nodded to two troopers; they filled some fire buckets and scattered the contents impartially between Joe Kerry and the two brothers.

When Gannon came back, they were standing, but none too steadily. He said, 'Kerry, you still want to nose around our goods?'

The man said nothing for a moment, then he shook his head, searched around for his fallen hat, then picked it up and jammed it on his head. 'Maybe I'll see you in the wild-horse country,' he said.

'Don't come looking for us,' Ben Clayton warned. 'We was just havin' fun tonight.'

Kerry lingered a moment longer as though

he were searching for something to say, then he wheeled and walked away, the two brothers following him. Gannon spoke to the sergeant of the guard. 'We're going to bunk in the stable. Captain Anders' permission.'

'It's all right with me,' the sergeant said and put his men back on their duty. Gannon and Clayton went inside, pitched down some fresh hay and spread their blankets.

Gannon said, 'Ben, you ought not brag so much.' The young man looked surprised, as though he didn't know what Gannon was talking about. And Gannon explained. 'Well, you know, that remark you made to Kerry about this just being for fun tonight.' He shook his head. 'Damned if I see it was fun.'

'That's because you was on the bottom,' Ben said.

Gannon took offense and said, 'Now don't start telling me how you licked all three of 'em.'

Ben Clayton laughed as he spoke. 'Well, I did, Charlie. How can you get around it?'

'All right!' Gannon snapped. 'The next time I'll step back and let you do it without anyone getting in the road!' He settled himself on his blankets and lay there, aching in body, his head throbbing. 'Let's not say any more about it, huh, Ben?'

'It suits me,' Clayton said. He sat down and took off his boots. 'You know, that Joe Kerry's going to take us a lot more seriously the next

43

time.'

'I don't want there to be a next time,' Gannon said. 'I'd rather get along with a man than fight.' He lay in silence for a time. 'How's your head feel, Ben?'

'It aches,' Clayton admitted. 'Why?'

'Mine aches too,' Gannon said. 'But not so bad I can't get out of here.' He turned his head and looked at Ben Clayton. 'I don't know what Joe Kerry's thinking, but tomorrow, when we're clear of the post, I'll be lookin' for him behind every rock.'

'So let's not wait for tomorrow, huh?'

'My notion exactly,' Gannon said. He got up. 'I'll go see the captain and ask if it's all right for us to leave by the side gate. You harness up.'

'I'll meet you there,' Ben promised and turned to get the horses out of the stalls. Gannon crossed the parade to Anders' quarters and hesitated a moment before knocking because the place was dark. He rapped on the door and heard Anders get out of bed. The door opened a crack and Anders squinted out.

'Oh, Gannon. I wondered who it was at this hour. It must be nine o'clock.'

'My partner and I are leaving tonight, Captain.' Then he told Anders about the fight and the captain listened and nodded.

'Well, it's smart to keep the jump on Joe Kerry,' Anders said. He turned inside and lit

44

the lamp, then wrote a note and handed it to Charlie Gannon. 'You give this to the guard at the south gate and he'll let you out with no trouble.' He offered his hand. 'Good luck.'

'Thanks. We may see you on our way back,' Gannon said, and returned to the stable. He hadn't expected Ben Clayton to have finished harnessing, but the rig and Clayton were gone and Gannon walked around the remount corral to the back gate, wondering where that young fella got all his vinegar.

The corporal took the note, squinted at it, and passed them through. After the gates closed, they cut around in a loose circle and established a proper direction.

'I feel some better,' Ben Clayton said. 'Like the day I ran away from home.' He turned and peered through the darkness at Gannon. 'Did you run away or get kicked out?'

'Now that you mention it, I guess it was kicked. As I recall, Pa came up to me one day and said, "Son, you're gettin' a little too big fer six in a bed. Why don't you go up the line a hunnert miles or so and get yourself a job?"' Gannon laughed softly. 'I did, too. Never went back. Pa was pretty final when he said a thing.'

'I'm not going back either,' Ben Clayton said. 'Ma's probably had two or three more kids I don't even know about. Maybe someday a fella will come up to me and say, "Mr. Clayton, I'm your brother." And you know what, I ain't even going to give a damn.'

45

'You'd care,' Gannon said. 'There's blood in us, boy, not skimmed milk. We all care.'

'Damned if I do,' Clayton repeated. 'You and I are friends, Charlie. That's all I've got. And I don't want any more.'

'You will,' Gannon said. 'Yeah, you will.'

They camped out the night in the rocks four miles north of the post, and it was unpleasant, cold, and silent, and the dawn came with a push of raw wind and later the sun seemed to have no heat, being filtered through a high gauze of clouds.

All that day they moved steadily, and Charlie Gannon never once shook the notion that Joe Kerry and his friends were not too far behind them. He tried, when he could, to stay into the high country, and toward evening of the second day they dry camped in a rocky upthrust, hiding the team and loaded buckboard and picking for a sleeping ground a very high place that commanded a wide view of their back trail.

Darkness was several hours away. They had camped early, too early. But Gannon wanted a look behind him, and Ben Clayton didn't argue the point. Both of them lay belly flat, having their look, then Ben reached out and tugged Gannon's pants leg. Turning his head, Gannon saw the gila monster six or eight yards away, squatting on a flat rock, button eyes fixed in a hypnotic gaze upon them.

Ben turned over and leveled his rifle, and

Gannon's hand came out just in time to prevent the hammer from falling.

'You want to call the neighbors?' he asked softly.

Ben hadn't been thinking and an embarrassed look came over his face. He put the rifle down and Gannon picked up a small rock, gave it a light toss, and the bounce of it made the gila monster scamper away.

'Those damned things are poison,' Ben said.

'Yep. So's Kerry, once he heard that shot. Don't forget the Indians, huh?' He reached out and tapped his knuckles against Ben's forehead. 'Use that, huh?'

Ben grinned and made a face, but Gannon knew it was a lesson. Clayton didn't like to be caught off balance that way; he took a big pride in doing a thing right, and when he was caught wrong it bothered him.

They went on watching, and time passed. It seemed a very long time to them. Then Gannon coughed slightly to draw Ben's attention, and pointed far back on their trail. Three horsemen moved slowly, with George in the lead, picking up the sign; neither of them doubted their purpose.

'I guess they don't think we've camped for the night yet,' Ben Clayton said.

'Likely not, which was what I wanted them to think. They'll come right up on us sudden like.'

'Now I don't like that,' Clayton said. 'They

don't want to talk, Charlie.'

'Yeah, that's so,' Gannon said, squinting his eyes. 'Well, I thought I'd open the conversation with this, say at around a hundred yards.' He patted the receiver of his Winchester. He turned his head and looked at Ben Clayton. The young man was somber-faced. 'Did you ever shoot at a man, Ben?'

'Can't say as I have,' Clayton admitted. 'You?'

'No, but like you always say, there's a first time for everything, huh?'

Ben didn't answer, just stayed still and watchful. Now and then Kerry and his friends disappeared from view, but they always popped up again, and always a little nearer.

The last stretch of trail they would have to climb was a narrow ribbon of rock that crested just below where Gannon and Clayton lay. Gannon said, 'I'd judge a hundred yards to be about halfway up. Wouldn't you say so?'

'I ain't very good at judgin' distance,' Clayton said. He fell silent a moment or two, then nudged Gannon. 'Are we going to just pick one and shoot?'

'Sure, I'll give you first choice.'

'Hell, I don't want first choice!' He frowned and went back to his study of the men coming slowly up the trail.

When they got to the bottom, Charlie Gannon said, 'Aim for the spot where the martingale ought to Y. I'll take Kerry's horse.'

His relief washed the strain from Clayton's eyes, and he smiled and swore softly at Gannon at the same time. They cradled their rifles and squinted along the octagonal barrels, and when the distance was right Charlie Gannon pulled the trigger.

Joe Kerry's horse reared and fell backward into Al's horse, then Kerry kicked free and struck the ground in a rolling tumble. George stopped and started to turn and Ben Clayton's .44 banged echoes through the hills and put George afoot.

The two men scrambled for cover, then thought of their rifles still on the saddles and Kerry made a dash for his. As he reached for it Gannon's bullet ripped leather and shattered the saddlehorn inches from Kerry's hand, and he forgot about the rifle and got behind a big rock.

Al was somewhere down the trail, clean out of sight, and the two men lay there for a time, content to wait.

Finally Joe Kerry yelled up, 'That's a fine way, just opening up on a man! We didn't mean you no harm!' Kerry's heavy voice reverberated and answered itself, and Charlie Gannon thumbed two fresh cartridges into the loading gate. When he called down no answer, Kerry shouted again. 'Well, come on and murder us! We can't defend ourselves!'

'They got pistols,' Ben said, as though outraged at this lie.

Gannon shook his head and made a soft shushing sound with his lips. He seemed perfectly content to lay there and look at the two dead horses.

'Al! Al!' Kerry's voice rattled like a pea in an empty tin cup. After another silence, he called up again. 'Our canteens are on the saddles! Let us get them!'

'Get 'em and clear out!' Gannon said flatly.

'No shooting now! We're coming out, unarmed!'

Gannon glanced at Ben Clayton and motioned with his hand and Clayton scurried off, keeping well hidden among the rocks, but circling back to get around and behind Kerry in case one of them tried a flanking movement.

'Can we come out?' Kerry called up. 'I want your word, Gannon!'

'I'll think about it,' Gannon said. He wanted to buy a little time for Ben Clayton.

He let a few minutes pass. From across the rock-screened trail he heard a man grunt in surprise, then it sounded like someone had dropped a honeydew melon. George sprawled into view, tumbled down once and struck the dusty trail and lay still. Ben Clayton stood up and raised his rifle over his head.

'All right,' Gannon said. 'Get the canteens, and come up and get your friend.'

Kerry exposed himself. He had taken off his pistol belt as a display of innocence, obviously hoping that George would take care of things

50

from around behind. When Kerry saw George sprawled in the trail with a knot on the back of his head, he made a reach for the rifle, still in the scabbard, but Gannon's shout stopped him.

'I'll bust your arm!' He stood up then, in full view of Kerry. 'Take the water and light out. Leave the guns. By the time you get to Fort Defiance and get more horses and back here, we'll be long gone. Leave it that way and live awhile.'

'Next time,' Kerry said, 'I'll be more careful.'

'You should be,' Gannon told him.

Ben came back with George's bone-handled pistol and a belt of shells; he seemed proud of the trophy, but Gannon expressed no interest. Kerry got the canteens, and George struggled to his feet. Then they lurched down the back trail and finally passed from view.

'Go down and get the rifles and see if you can find Kerry's six-shooter,' Gannon said. He sat down on a rock and waited until Ben Clayton came back. He emptied the rifles, then smashed them to uselessness. The pistol belonging to Kerry was likewise damaged, but when he asked for the one Ben had taken off George, the young man balked.

'I'll keep this one.'

'It's just excess weight,' Gannon said. 'We can use the shells, and that's all.'

'Now look,' Clayton said flatly. 'Since I consider this my property, suppose I decide,

51

huh?'

'This is the first time you've ever come out and said a thing was yours or mine, and not ours,' Charlie Gannon said. 'But I suppose there's a first time for that, too.'

'I'm getting tired of hearing you say that,' Ben said sternly. Then he blew out his cheeks and expelled the breath in a whistle between his tight-pressed lips. 'Charlie, what the hell we arguing about?'

'We'd better quit it,' Gannon said gravely. 'I guess every Indian in thirty miles heard those shots.'

It was a thought that had not yet occurred to Ben Clayton, but now that he thought of it, he found it very sobering. So much so that he voiced no objection at all to moving the camp for the night.

CHAPTER FOUR

The darkness was split by a ragged finger of lightning, and an instant later a rock-shaking clap of thunder shook up a storm of echoes through the hills. Charlie Gannon turned his face upward as the first of the rain fell, and he said, 'Been kind of expecting it since we had that muddy-lookin' sky the other day.' He reached for his ground cloth and pulled it around his blankets.

For the last five hours they had been stumbling along in the darkness, feeling their way along the faint trail and dragging brush behind the buckboard to wipe out their tracks. Now the rain would finish the job; they wouldn't have to worry about the Indians finding them so easily.

They spent a cold, damp night and woke to a gray, drizzling day. The clouds were low-hanging, full of unspent moisture, completely hiding all the high ridges and peaks. With two rifle barrels tied together and a tarp wrapped around to form a rain break, Gannon built a small fire, using the lid from a wooden box for fuel. Over this small blaze they cooked their first hot meal since leaving Fort Defiance, and it wasn't much—some fried backfat, a skillet of beans, and some coffee. Then the fire was put out with the knowledge that the rain would wash all trace of it away in a day.

The rain didn't last long; it fizzled out during the next afternoon, and by nightfall the low clouds were gone and stars shone bright in the clean dark sky. By degrees the land changed, opening into stretches of desert with buttes rising high and flat-topped.

A day of this, and Gannon made the decision to swing west. Water was scarce but the game trails and the horse trails, which both men watched for, led them to it. Twice in three days they saw horses, herds of them, far off, raising a plume of dust in the still air.

'This is it,' Gannon said, smiling.

'Sure looks it,' Clayton agreed. 'You suppose this is the country Kerry got run out of?' He kept swinging his head from side to side, having his look, but understanding that in a lifetime he would never see all of it; it was that immense. The buttes stood like sentinels, brown and weathered with multi-shaded lines running horizontally through them as though they were built up of huge slabs of wood. Between them lay desert with stunted brush and a brown fine sand eroded off the stone buttes.

As they traveled they saw dust devils rise up from the desert floor, and at times they were hard put to make out whether this was caused by the wind, or horses, or Indians.

The going was easier though, more level, but it wasn't an easy country. In the evening they camped near one of the buttes, and saw how deceiving they were from a distance. The sides were not smooth, and they did not rise cleanly from the desert. Instead, rock jumble cluttered about them and some had clefts and canyons in their flanks.

Ben Clayton said, 'Man, this is sure wild-horse country, ain't it?'

'Wild Indian country, too,' Gannon said. 'I wish I knew where we are.'

'I'm lost too,' Clayton said. 'But I don't mind it. From what I can see of this country, a man'd be lost even if he knew where he was.'

'A sage observation,' Gannon admitted and started kicking some of the smaller rocks aside so he could clear a camp. 'It don't seem like much sense to me to keep on going, Ben. We've been on the move almost a month now, unless I'm countin' one week twice. Likely we'll find a better place than this, somewhere near water, but it shouldn't take more than a day or two to do that.'

His mind was making plans, the way it always did when he fell so silent. Hardly two words passed between them that night, and after Ben Clayton was asleep, Charlie Gannon lay there, looking at the stars and figuring out all the things that would have to be done.

Gannon knew how to catch wild horses; he'd been doing it off and on for years, but still he sorted out each detail as though afraid he would make a mistake somewhere through an oversight.

Wild-horse country was nearly always full of high places, a dry land with waterholes few and far between. It was always country that was tough on a man, hot in the summer, cold in the winter. Catching wild horses was just about the workingest job a man could tackle, and to succeed he needed craft and a good deal of luck, along with the stamina of an antelope and the patience of a saint.

Gannon worried about some of these things. He knew the business all right. He was as patient as a man could be, and somehow or other he managed to swelter through the summers, although they sapped his strength, and shiver through the winters, even when the cold left an ache in his bones. It was just that he could feel the steam going out of him, the old vinegar finding it harder to come up when that extra effort was called for.

Like when he'd been mixing it up with Kerry. Gannon had wanted badly to put the man down, then turn to one of the others and whip him good so that afterward he could say, 'I took care of two-thirds of 'em.' Then Ben Clayton would know and keep it in mind that old Charlie could pull his end of the rope.

Only it hadn't come out that way. Kerry's punches had hurt him, more than he remembered from the last fight he'd had. And damn it, when Kerry put him down it was nigh impossible to get back up. All he could do was wrestle the man and hope for the wind to come back, the strength to return so his muscles would do what his mind wanted.

Gannon told himself that if Ben had held off another minute or two, he'd have been all right, and he'd have whippped Joe Kerry. That was a good thought to hang on to, but it was dimmed somewhat by the knowledge that even if it had turned out that way, he'd still have only won a third of the fight.

He tried, but could not quite still the resentment he felt, the suspicion he had that while he pretended to make the decisions, to lead the way, it was really Ben Clayton who was doing it.

The next morning they saddled two horses, and riding the buckboard and goods, rode out to scout out horse trails and waterholes within a ten-mile circle. What Gannon wanted was really a seep of some kind, not big enough to attract a horse herd, but enough to keep them in water. He found such a place over near the next butte; the seep was well hidden, a good place for a camp, especially if they built a fire only at night so the smoke wouldn't show and attract Indians.

And the camp would be a good four miles from the nearest horse trails and water, which was as it should be; a green horse hunter could move in too close and booger every horse in the country.

It was late afternoon when Gannon and Clayton started back after their buckboard and spare horses. They saw dust several times and argued back and forth as to what caused it, wild horses, the wind, or Indians. A couple of times, Ben swore it was smoke, but Gannon didn't think so, and said so firmly enough to end the discussion.

He wasn't going to be spooked by every rise of dust he saw, not when they were going to spend the winter here. If a man started that he'd be all nerves in thirty days, not good for anything, like a whip-broke horse.

The buttes were casting giant shadows when

they drew near last night's camp. The air was still, completely hushed, and Gannon figured that if he let out one big long yell it would be heard for forty miles at least.

Perhaps because he was thinking about how quiet it was, his mind was sensitive to sound, for he suddenly held out his hand and stopped, cocking his head to one side. He heard it then, a box being smashed open, and a mutter of angry voices. Quickly he dismounted, taking his rifle with him, and Ben Clayton did the same. They trail-reined their horses in a cluster of rocks and went on afoot, making no noise, but working high so they could end up over their camp.

Finally they came to a crest of rocks and looked down. Five Piute Indians were ransacking the buckboard, digging into everything, scattering their goods all over the ground.

Gannon leveled his rifle and fired into the rise at their feet, and while the echo of the shot slammed and clattered about, the Indians turned this way and that, trying to figure out where it had come from.

'What're you doing there!' Gannon yelled down. He was hidden from their view and the echo of his voice effectively masked his position.

The Indians started to stir, and he shot again, into the rocks this time so that the bullet spanged and whined around.

'Stand still!' he shouted, and they did as they were told.

'Whiskey!' one said. 'Where whiskey!'

'There's no whiskey! Go on, get out of here!' He levered off two more fast rounds to get them mounted, then he moved in case someone saw a trace of powder smoke and tried to do something about this clue to his position.

They were not, he saw, looking for a fight. Just a drink, and he couldn't figure out why they thought he'd be carrying whiskey, unless they had taken the notion that all white men drank. Ben, without being told what to do, scooted around so that he was placed on the quarter to Gannon, and there he watched the Indians take their final departure. They were a scrubby lot, half-naked, badly armed; one carried a flintlock rifle to scare his enemies, for he had no flint in it to make it shoot.

Storming away in a cloud of dust, yipping like molested dogs, they struck out across the desert floor, and the two horse hunters came down from their rocky perches.

Ben looked at the scatter and said, 'They made a mess of this, for dang sure.'

'Anything missing?'

'How can you tell with all this stuff scattered around?' He kicked one pile of rope; they had broken open the huge coil, presenting him with a tedious job of rewinding. He poked around until he found two lanterns, lit them, and hung

59

them on some shovels jabbed solidly into the ground. Night was coming on fast, and in the last bland cast of light, the lanterns seemed to glow bright yellow.

'Let's eat first,' Gannon said and put together a small fire.

'Might as well build that up,' Clayton suggested. The Indians know we're here, and we're going to move in the morning anyway.'

'All right,' Gannon said and wondered why he didn't think of that. It galled him a little, to have Ben come on with a good idea like that. More and more he was showing a tendency to do things on his own, like in the rocks just now, he went off and flanked the Indians without a motion or nothing. Suppose, Gannon thought, I hadn't wanted him to do that. He'd probably have done it anyway.

After eating, they began to restore their goods to order and repack the buckboard. They had a lot of stuff there and it had to go on just so or not go on at all.

Even though the night was cool, Gannon worked up a good sweat and he kept looking at Ben Clayton to see if he was sweating. It pleased Gannon when he saw that the young man was.

They worked hard and pretty late, and they both paid so much attention to what they were doing that they forgot where they were. Ben Clayton was stretching the tarp over the load when he stopped suddenly and spoke to

Charlie Gannon.

'Did you hear anything?'

Gannon thought a minute. If he said yes, and there wasn't anything, he'd look pretty foolish. And if he said no, he'd be plain admitting that Ben's ears were sharper than his own.

But then the whole matter was taken out of their hands when a woman said, 'You heard something all right. Just stand still. I've got a shotgun here.' There was a rustling of cloth as she came closer to the out-spread ring of lamplight. And there was someone with her, for she said, 'Get their rifles, Beans. Walk around me, boy, not in front of me!'

Both men turned their heads, then a boy of seven or eight came up and took their Winchesters. He had a round, well-fed face, and the most harmless smile, as though he loved everyone and was terribly sorry he had to do this.

When the rifles were safely out of reach, the woman came forward, pressed the muzzle of the shotgun into Ben Clayton's back, and lifted the bone-handled pistol from his holster. She gave it a toss backward and they heard it plop in the dust somewhere out there in the dark.

'All right, you can turn around now,' she said.

They did, slowly, so as not to excite her, get her to do something foolish, like pulling the trigger. She stood near the outer edge of the

61

lamplight, a rather tall woman, in her late twenties, with a plain, determined face. Pleasant though, Gannon thought. Her hair seemed brown; he really couldn't tell in that light. She had good bones and he could see that work didn't frighten her, for her hands were rough, and the sun had darkened her skin. Her eyes were wide-spaced, and unafraid. He supposed the shotgun gave her that courage.

'Who are you, lady?' Charlie Gannon asked. He was conscious of his appearance, dirty-faced and needing a shave. Then he tried a smile. Hell, it couldn't hurt anything. But he did not see her expression change. She did not accept his offer at friendliness.

'It doesn't matter who I am,' she said. 'I suppose you sold the whiskey to the Indians. I've been waiting for you two to come back. This time I swore I'd catch you.'

'Lady,' Ben said pleadingly, 'we've never been here before, and we sold no whiskey. Didn't you hear the shooting?'

'I did.'

'We drove the Indians off,' Gannon said. 'They had our goods scattered all over the ground.'

The woman looked at the neatly loaded buckboard, then said, 'Did they now? It hardly looks like it.' She made a small motion with the shotgun. 'All right, unload it. Every last stick of it.'

'Why, what for?' Ben asked.

'Because if you didn't give the Piutes any whiskey, then you still must have it.' She spoke in a strong, clear voice, and Gannon wondered what he could say to talk her out of this.

He took off his hat and threw it on the ground in annoyance. 'Lady, what do you want to do this for? Say, ain't you a Mormon?'

'I am.'

Gannon smiled. 'Well, then ain't it against your religion to be threatenin' us with that shotgun?'

'There's nothing in the Bible about shootin' varmints,' she said.

He still retained the smile; he hoped it would disarm her. 'Lady, would you really shoot?'

She answered him by pulling the trigger and scattering buckshot into the dust before his feet. Gannon jumped back quickly as though something had bitten him and saw that his hat, which had been lying on the ground, was torn to shreds.

'Let's unload, huh, Charlie?'

They worked like eager slaves, placing everything on the ground so she could see, and she stood there all the time, expecting to turn up the jugs at any moment. Finally when there was nothing left but the canteens and water keg, she insisted on sniffing them. Then she looked at each of them and the muzzle of her shotgun sagged. 'I guess you never had the whiskey. Those few Piutes couldn't have lugged off a wagon load of it. And you ain't been in this country long enough to get to the main camp. I—I've made a mistake, I think.'

'Lady,' Charlie Gannon said, 'you sure as hell have.'

'Well you don't have to swear!'

'No, I guess I don't. I guess I ought to thank you for comin' along and shootin' my forty-dollar hat to pieces. Well, I paid that for it ten years back.' He felt compelled to keep this honest; she was the kind to remember a man's innocent lies. 'I guess I ought to be grateful for you makin' us work like dogs just to prove something we told you wasn't so all along. Can you give me one good reason why I shouldn't take that shotgun away from you and turn you over my knee?'

'Don't you dare. For the last couple of years now, white men have sold whiskey to the Indians. Well, not over in this part of the country yet, but I heard the Indians say there was going to be some brought in.'

'Who's going to bring it?' Ben Clayton asked.

'I don't know who or I wouldn't have bothered you.'

'Oh, we weren't bothered,' Gannon said. 'We always load and unload our rig twice a night.'

'I'm dreadfully sorry, believe me.' She was contrite now. The boy, who had been standing

64

there all the while, brought their rifles back, set them exactly where he'd found them and slipped Ben Clayton's pistol back into his holster.

'You're a good boy, Beans,' Gannon said, and got a quick, sincere smile.

'He's young,' the woman said. 'He can't tell good from bad yet.'

'Too bad he's got to learn,' Gannon said softly. 'Would you mind telling us who told you that white men were selling whiskey?'

'The Indians told me,' she said. 'Say, if you'd fix up a fire, I'll make some coffee.'

Gannon looked at Clayton, then the young man put one together. He got out the coffee and bucket and filled it full of water before placing it on the fire.

'I asked you once who you was,' Gannon said. 'You feel like telling me now?'

'Jenny Regan,' she said. 'This is my boy, Beans.'

'Funny name for a kid,' Ben said frankly. 'I thought all you Mormons named kids after somebody in the Bible.'

'Was he of my own flesh, I guess I would have,' Jenny Regan said. 'The Piutes traded him from the Apaches. When my Adam brought him home, he remarked that he wasn't much bigger than a bag of beans. The baby laughed, so the name just stuck.'

'Adam?' Gannon asked. He never knew it to fail; all the good-looking women had men.

'He's dead. Two years, goin' on. Piutes killed him.'

'And you still talk to 'em?' Gannon asked.

'They were drunk,' she said. 'A man ain't accountable when he's drunk, especially an Indian.'

'There must be somethin' to this love your neighbor stuff, Charlie,' Ben said.

'Appears that way,' he said.

Jenny Regan moved closer to the fire, now that the water was beginning to thump in the can. The boy stood there, holding the enormous shotgun, and she hunkered down, measuring the coffee in her cupped hand. Without looking at Gannon, she said, 'I'm sorry about your hat, mister.'

'Gannon—Charlie Gannon.'

'I'll replace it, Mr. Gannon,' she said.

'Well, now that's not necessary at all.'

'My Adam had a good hat. You come to my place and I'll give it to you. It's the right thing, so do it.' She pointed to the northwest. 'You go eight or so miles across the desert to twin buttes. You can't miss it.'

'I can get along without a hat,' Gannon said.

'Oh, it ain't your head I'm thinking of,' she said honestly. 'It's my conscience.' She looked at him then and he thought she had fine eyes and a fine, strong face with good bones and a skin the sun hadn't been able to ruin. 'I'm not a very good Mormon, I guess. More often than not I put my own soul first, then think of the other fella.' She spoke of this as though it were a private sin that she was working very hard on, but one on which she had made little progress.

'You live out here alone?' Ben asked.

'I've got Beans,' Jenny said. She looked more closely at Ben Clayton, and the bone-handled gun he carried. 'Seems to me I've seen that pistol before.'

'I took it off one of Kerry's friends,' Clayton said, the brag strong in his voice, and Gannon could see that she didn't like that sort of thing in a man and it made him feel good all over.

'That's where I saw it,' she said. 'The big one had it.' Her eyes still held the question as to how he came to have it, but she wasn't the nosey kind.

Well, Gannon thought, Ben will tell her. He'll have to brag.

And he did, not leaving out a thing. When he finished, he stood there as though expecting her to admire him, but she didn't. She said, 'Anybody can sneak up behind a man. I did, remember?'

He remembered and his face took on color. He sat down then and leaned against the buckboard wheel. Gannon was squatting by the fire. He glanced at her now and then, then took the hot coffee off so it could cool a little.

'We're going to change our camp,' he said. 'Those Indians will come back.'

'They won't bother you,' Jenny said, 'if you come to my place.'

Gannon frowned. 'How's that?'

'If they see your sign leading up to and away from my place, they won't bother you,' she repeated. 'I'm friendly with them, and they respect that.'

'Well, I don't like buyin' my peace from a woman,' he said.

'We all have to buy it from someone,' she pointed out, and he didn't have an argument for that. 'You're horse hunters?'

Gannon nodded.

'There are lots of horses here,' Jenny said. 'But you're starting late in the year. When Kerry came that time, it was in the spring.'

'We're going to winter out here,' Clayton said.

'Why, that's wonderful,' she said, quite delighted. 'My near neighbor is thirty miles and I was afraid all I'd have to talk to would be Piutes who came around to beg. The winter's hard on them, you know.'

'Jenny,' Gannon said, boldly using her first name. 'How come you stay?'

'I've got a farm.'

'Yes, but I mean, with your husband dead and all, I'd think—'

She shook her head. 'The church sent us here, and I'll stay until I'm told to leave. You don't understand that, do you?'

Gannon grinned and scratched his head. 'No, I always do what I please.'

Her eyes fascinated him, so serious, yet so

68

warm and alive. 'Do you really?' Then she laughed and reached for the coffee, pouring it into the tin cups. They sipped it, for it was very hot, then she said, 'I'm going to have to stay the night. It took me nearly all day to get here after I saw the smoke.'

Ben Clayton laughed. 'So it *was* smoke I saw. Maybe the next time you'll listen to me, huh, Charlie?'

'Maybe, if I think it looks like smoke.' He looked at Jenny Regan. 'How did you find our camp?'

'I told you, from the smoke. Then I heard the shots.' She regarded him with some amusement, then laughed. 'Does it really pinch to admit a woman could do that?'

'Well, not every woman,' Gannon said. 'That's for dang sure.'

She finished her coffee and tossed the grounds away. 'I hate to ask, but could you spare two blankets? It's much too late for us to start back tonight.'

'Get them some blankets, Ben,' Gannon said. Then he looked at her. 'Aren't you afraid, staying here with two strange men?'

She smiled and accepted the blankets Clayton offered, then she rolled up into one, and the boy did the same. 'No, I'm not afraid,' she said, and lay back, her eyes closed, her hands folded on her chest. And Charlie Gannon sat there a moment, looking at her, and he guessed she was right. Nothing was

69

going to hurt her; she had no reason to be afraid.

CHAPTER FIVE

Harry Graves' arrival at Fort Defiance was somewhat of a blessing to the officers of the post who were getting tired of each other's conversation and each other's poker playing. Graves arrived on one of the infrequent stages; only four out of ten ever came through from Lordsburg unmolested by the Apaches.

All the passengers were put up in quarters along officers' row and ate in the officers' mess. Graves met Captain Anders there, got to talking and was invited into a card game, which was really the only pastime permitted an officer at Fort Defiance.

Usually they played in a side room at the sutlers' place, within handy stepping distance to the bar, yet far enough away so as not to be bothered by the run of customers. Graves played a clean, calm game, bet modestly out of consideration for the limited purses he would like to empty, and seemed to lose more than he won. However this was only an illusion; he was steadily drawing ahead, taking a few dollars here and there.

The four officers playing with him were strangers. He was content to leave it that way.

They sprinkled their game with talk, which annoyed him since poker was serious business to him. He generally stayed clear of the talk, but without appearing unsociable.

Around eleven o'clock three men came into the sutlers, loudly demanded a bottle and glasses, then turned to the side room and the poker game.

Captain Anders turned his head briefly and glanced at them, then said, 'I thought you'd left the post, Kerry.'

'As you can see, we came back,' Joe Kerry said. His clothes were dusty, and when Anders glanced at his boots, it seemed that they had done an uncommon amount of walking.

'I take it you got what you went after,' Anders said dryly.

Kerry mumbled something with the glass to his mouth, and George and Al Manners just looked at each other. When this hand was finished, three of the officers got up, and Anders registered surprise.

'Quitting?'

'Early duty,' one said. 'Thanks for an interesting evening, Mr. Graves.'

'You're welcome,' Graves said. He looked at Kerry and the two brothers. 'The chairs are still warm, gentlemen. Perhaps they left a little luck behind, too.'

'I'm sure as hell not having any,' Kerry said, sitting down. He motioned for the Manners brothers to do the same, and took the deal from Harry Graves.

'You look like foot soldiers,' Captain Anders said, a faint smile making his mustache rise on the ends. 'Your horses go lame?'

'Very funny,' Kerry said sourly.

Harry Graves maintained a neutral expression, but he was curious; he didn't like vague talk going on at his table. 'I like a good joke,' he said invitingly.

Joe Kerry's glance touched his briefly. 'This isn't a funny story, mister.' He turned to Captain Anders. 'I could blame you because you opened the side gate for 'em.'

Anders shrugged to indicate that he didn't care what they thought, or who they blamed. He bet and accepted his cards. 'Gannon was under no obligation to wait until morning,' he said. 'Kerry, he might have had good reason to mistrust you. You did try to waylay them, didn't you?'

'Now just a minute!' Kerry snapped. 'I've staked out that country, and if a man takes a horse there it's the same as rustling to me.'

Harry Graves was listening with a sharper attention now; he held his cards in his hands as though he had forgotten he had them. Then Graves tipped back his head and laughed and Kerry looked at him resentfully.

'Just what the hell do you think is funny?' he asked.

Graves pulled his laughter down to a chuckle, then said, 'It's kind of nice to find

72

someone who learned about Charlie Gannon the hard way. The next time, we'll both be more careful.'

After studying Graves a moment Anders said, 'Somewhere in my mind rattled around the notion that no one got off at Fort Defiance without a good reason.' He tossed his cards on the table and slid back his chair. 'You—ah, gentlemen will want to talk now, with so much in common, and I don't want to hear it. Good night, and lousy luck.'

Joe Kerry took offense at this. He snapped, 'Can't the army keep its mind on the Indians?'

'I'm trying,' Anders said. 'But now that you brought it up, Kerry, I might say that we'd have less trouble with the Indians if we had less horse hunters. About three less.'

After he left, Harry Graves said, 'He doesn't like you, Mr. Kerry.'

'I don't want to marry him either,' Kerry said. He folded his big hands and looked at Graves. 'Suppose you tell me why you're here?'

'You tell me about Gannon,' Graves said, smiling. 'You tell me your story and I'll tell you mine.'

Kerry did, not leaving out anything, but smoothing over his intentions with a quickly manufactured logic. Graves wasn't amused now; he listened with a rapt attention, and when Kerry was through Graves filled him in on the unpleasantness in Lordsburg. Then he

73

leaned back in his chair and asked, 'Don't you think we have a lot in common?'

'We do,' Kerry said. 'If Gannon and that kid think we're not going after them again, they're crazy.' He tapped his finger hard against the table top. 'Graves, we've put in time and money, and got the Indians to work with us. Do you blame me for getting sore?'

'No,' Graves said. 'I'm a little sore myself, from riding that pole. Can you use a fourth man?'

Kerry looked at him and tried to judge beneath the suit of clothes, tried to measure him for what he was. Then he nodded, 'All right. We're going to leave in the morning. I don't suppose you have a horse?'

'No, I haven't. Damned little luggage.'

'We can outfit you,' Kerry said, settling the matter. He took a Moonshine Crook from his pocket and put a match to it. 'I know the country north of here like the back of my hand. I figure to find 'em, fix 'em, and be back here in a week.'

'I hear the Piutes are worth looking out for,' Graves said.

Kerry smiled. 'We'll take care of that. About four gallons' worth.'

Graves made a brief appreciative gesture with his lips, then shuffled and dealt the cards. 'I'll bet five dollars,' he said. 'Five card stud.'

'A wonderful game,' Kerry admitted and puffed his cigar.

74

While he peeked at his hole card, Graves glanced at George and Al Manners. 'Don't they ever say anything?'

'Nothing that I can't say better,' Joe Kerry said. 'I don't like a man who's all mouth.'

*　　　*　　　*

Charlie Gannon just couldn't see the sense of going to Jenny Regan's place, but she was so firm about it that he went along to prevent argument. To Ben Clayton it really didn't make any difference; he was as non-resistant as the desert dust, shoved by every fickle wind that came along.

Jenny had her own horse and the boy, Beans, had ridden double with her, but on the way to her place he wanted to ride with Gannon. Never having had contact with children before, Gannon put up with it in silence, and rode along, the boy bobbing up and down on the horse's rump, the small fingers tightly hooked into the belt loops of his jeans. It seemed a little odd to him that he had never talked to a child, never held one on his knee, that he could remember. In his life they were just noise running down a street, or something hiding behind their mother's dress when strangers called.

She lived by a spring and there were trees in her yard. Ben took the horses to the small barn and Jenny went on in, motioning for Charlie

Gannon to follow her. The rooms were small, but as neat as he had ever seen. Most of the furniture was handmade; her husband had been a craftsman, capable and thorough. Gannon could tell at a glance that the things her husband had built were meant to last a hundred years; there was that finality in his touch.

Right away she went to the closet and brought out a hat. It was black, with a round crown and a straight brim. She handed it to Charlie Gannon. 'He only wore it to church; it was his praying hat, Mr. Gannon. I want you to have it, and no argument.'

'Well, I surely thank you,' he said and held it, twirling it between his blunt fingers.

'Please sit down.' He hesitated, then took a chair at the table, and carefully placed the hat to one side; he didn't think it was right to put it on the floor, since it had been Regan's praying hat and all.

Ben and the boy came in and when Ben saw the hat, he laughed and said, 'Well, if it ain't Parson Gannon. You out savin' souls today?'

'Shut up, Ben,' Gannon said curtly, and silently cursed him for being thoughtless.

Jenny didn't seem to think anything of it. She said, 'Mr. Gannon, if you like, you could put a crease in the crown and roll the brim a little so that it—'

'I like it fine this way,' Charlie said quickly. He turned to the boy. 'Come on over here, son,

76

and let me have a look at you. Say, you're goin' to be a big fella all right. You have a pony to ride?'

Beans shook his head. 'I can't catch one.'

Jenny Regan laughed softly. 'The poor tyke's been trying to run one down. Can you imagine that?'

'They run too fast,' Beans said seriously. 'And their mamas are mean.'

'Well, we'll get you a pony,' Charlie Gannon said in a sudden burst of sympathy. 'I'll keep my eye out for one, and one of these days I'll lead him right up to the door.'

'You don't have to go to that bother,' Jenny said. 'It's only a boy's want. He'll outgrow it.'

'She's got a point there, Charlie,' Ben said quickly. He didn't approve of Gannon's generosity. 'Besides, by the time we get our trap built and a herd lined up, snow'll be starting to fly.'

Gannon glanced at Beans and found the boy's attention swinging from one to the other as the dearest thing to his heart was ruthlessly being bandied about, and at any moment now his dreams and hopes could be casually dashed to pieces. Gannon didn't know what touched him, the round, innocent face, or the eyes, frightened, yet trusting, or the very soul of this child, clean and uncluttered by wrong, reaching out to touch his own. He reached out and put his hand on the boy's shoulder and said, 'Son, I'll get you a pony, you hear?'

77

The smile was quick and full of relief and Gannon felt so good that he just couldn't bear to share it with anyone, so he tipped his head forward and made a big business of rolling a cigaret.

Jenny said, 'You'll stay and eat, won't you?'

'We ought to get back and tend to our goods,' Ben said. 'The Indians came once, and likely they'll come back.'

She shook her head. 'They won't bother your things now,' she said. They wanted to believe her; it would solve a lot of their problems if she was right, but it sounded too good to be true. Their expressions said so. 'I mean it. The Indians won't bother your things now. They'll see the tracks I made and know I stayed the night in your camp and understand that I've accepted you in this country.'

'You mean,' Ben said, 'that if you didn't accept us we'd be in for trouble?' He sounded as though his manly pride had been trampled on.

'Well, the Piutes trust me,' Jenny said. 'I give them some of the things I raise here on this little farm. And they do things for me.' This answer wasn't satisfying Ben Clayton; it was too soft, too kind. He wanted it straight out, so she gave it to him that way. 'I do mean that if I didn't accept you by some sign, the Indians would give you a lot of trouble. When Kerry came here some time back, I knew he was no good and wouldn't have anything to do with

78

him. The Piutes ran him out.'

'Well dog gone,' Ben said, 'I don't like to owe a woman.'

'We all owe someone,' Jenny said. 'Shanti, who is the chief of the Piutes, will come here to look at you. It's his way, and he means no harm. This house, simple as it is, is good medicine for them. I once saved Shanti's brother from sickness. They all know about it.' Then she smiled and Gannon thought that the room brightened considerably. 'You will stay for something to eat now, won't you?'

'Thank you,' Gannon said. 'We will.'

Even during the meal, Ben Clayton couldn't quite rid himself of the notion that he didn't need a woman to say whether he was good or not, acceptable or not, and Gannon, who knew his every mood and expression, could see how deeply bothered he was.

Jenny didn't seem to notice it, though. She talked freely about her journey to this land and her marriage to Adam Regan and how afraid she had been to come here, how she hid that fear from him until by some miracle it was gone. There had been no children; she'd been sorry about that, but it must have been God's will and she wouldn't question it.

The boy went out to play, then he came back in and said, 'Mum, Shanti's coming.'

'We'll have to go and greet him,' Jenny said. 'He'll be offended if we don't.' Her glance again touched the pistol Ben wore. 'I don't think he'll mind if you wear that, Mr. Clayton. But he may remember it and question it in his mind.'

'Take it off,' Gannon said. When Ben hesitated, Gannon added, 'You heard me, Ben!'

'Aw, don't be so proddy,' Clayton said and unbuckled the belt. He rolled it around the holster and Jenny put it in her clothes chest.

Then they went outside.

The Piutes were coming across the valley floor, nearly a dozen strong, with a bony, aged man in the lead. He wore only a skin around his loins, and had no weapons other than a knife at his belt.

They stopped and Shanti said, 'Fine day.'

'A truly fine day,' Jenny said. She gave Beans a shove. 'You may shake his hand.' And when the boy went forward she spoke softly, rapidly to Gannon and Clayton. 'His son is dead many years now. The boy was near Beans' age when it happened. In a way, I suppose he thinks of Beans as his own son; he's very fond of him.' Then she spoke to Shanti. 'Won't you get down? There is water for the horses of your people and a place at my table for you to sit.'

He accepted by dismounting with no change of expression. But Gannon, who watched him closely, saw how pleased the old chief was. Shanti, he suspected, was crowding sixty, yet he walked straight and his eyes were clear and strong; he was a man of dignity and character

80

for all his nakedness and obvious poverty.

When they went inside Jenny seated him at the table and put food before him, then motioned with her eyes for Gannon and Clayton to sit down.

'Shanti, these are new friends. Good men.' She smiled. 'They will bring Beans a pony soon.'

Gannon had never seen an Indian smile, and it was a surprising thing. 'Shake hands,' Shanti said mechanically, and pumped once, Indian-wise, as each offered a hand.

Jenny got up and brought a slate and chalk to the table. 'I've taught Shanti many things. He has also taught me, for he is wise.' She put the writing things before him. 'Will you write for our new friends, Shanti?'

The old man was like a child, Gannon thought, eager to show off before company. Not too neatly, he wrote: *I AM FREND*. Jenny clapped her hands and Gannon did the same because she wanted him to and Shanti sat there, all smiles.

'What's so great about that?' Ben Clayton asked.

Gannon took the slate and chalk and held them in his hands. 'Do you want to write something for him, Ben?'

'Now you know I can't write good,' Clayton said, embarrassed.

'Then shut up like a good boy,' Gannon warned, smiling all the while. 'Now you look at

81

what he wrote and applaud or I'll take your head off when we get back to camp.'

Ben regarded him for a minute, then applauded the words he could scarcely read.

Shanti's pleasure was complete. He ate with his fork, holding it clumsily, and Gannon could see that he preferred his fingers but would not use them because it might have offended Jenny Regan.

The boy came in and sat beside Shanti, and the old man put his arm around Beans' shoulder. Jenny bit her lips briefly, and said, 'Oh dear, now I'll have to soak his clothes in coal oil. Lice, you know.' She smiled at Shanti. 'You like? Good? Do you want more?'

He smiled and belched and shook his head. 'Go now,' he said. 'Shake hands.'

Again the pumping ritual took place, then he went out, proud and straight, with Beans by his side. A moment later they rode away and the boy came in, immediately shedding his clothes. It embarrassed Gannon a little to see the boy unabashed in his nakedness. Jenny got a tub and poured in two gallons of coal oil and plopped the clothes in, pushing them under with a short stick.

'Why do you let him in if he's got bugs?' Ben asked.

'Well, they're no bother unless you get close enough for them to pass from him to you.' Then she smiled. 'At least he bathes once or twice a year. I give them soap for Christmas.

The first time they ate it.' She gave Beans a smack on his peach-round bottom. 'Go get into your overalls, young man.'

Ben Clayton was standing there, looking at his right hand. 'You suppose—? I shook hands.'

Gannon had a hard time curbing his laughter. 'Why, Ben, you just hop right out of them clothes this instant!'

'Aw, you go to the devil,' Ben snapped and turned to the door. 'I'm going back to camp before there's any more foolishness around here.'

After he stomped out, Jenny Regan said, 'He's very young, isn't he?'

'Ben regards me as an old man with one foot in the grave,' Charlie Gannon said. 'And sometimes I think he ain't far off.' He picked up his hat from the table and stepped to the door. 'I'll ride back with Ben; we've been riding together for five years now.' He hesitated, as though wondering if what he had to say was proper or not. 'I don't suppose you leave the place much.'

'No, not much.'

He frowned. 'Ben and I are going to be busy, building traps and all. I guess it's too much to expect you to bring the boy over now and then.'

Her smile was faint, just a suggestion only. 'Would I be welcome if Beans wasn't along?'

'Oh, gosh, yes!' he said quickly. 'Well, you

know what I mean, Jenny.'

'Yes, I do know,' she said. 'It's a lonely country, Charlie. Sometimes I think I can't stand it another day. I want people around me; I need them. But I want good people. Is that too much to ask?'

'No, it ain't,' he said.

She always came out with what she wanted to know, and this surprised Gannon. 'Have you a woman, Charlie?'

'You mean, a wife?'

'No, a woman. There's a difference.'

He knew what she meant and shook his head. 'No woman, no wife. Been times though when I'd have settled for—'

'Yes,' she said, breaking in. 'In my thoughts I've had a hard time keeping man and husband separate, too.' Then she gave him her smile, that burst of brilliance that pushed aside all the trouble in her life, all the tears, and told him that no matter what happened, she was brave enough to go on. 'Good-bye, for now, Charlie. Don't be a stranger.'

'I'd get here,' he said, 'if my horse was dragging me the other direction.'

This was about the boldest thing he'd ever said to a woman, and he left quickly, circling the house to go to the barn. Ben was waiting with both horses, as though he knew Charlie would be along. He swung up and they rode out, and he turned one time to wave, then didn't look back again. He really didn't have to, for her face was an etching in his mind, a pleasant picture that he would enjoy seeing again and again.

Finally Ben said, 'You know, Charlie, I got to hand it to you.'

'Hand me what?' Gannon asked.

'Well, buttering her up that way, it was smart. Now we've got no Indian troubles at all. I like it.'

'You may not have Indian troubles,' Gannon said flatly, 'but you're getting plenty from me.'

Clayton snapped his head around and stared at him, then laughed. 'Oh, hell, you know how I meant it.'

'Yeah, and I didn't like it.'

They rode along until the Regan place was a smudge, then Gannon stopped his horse and got down. Ben Clayton stopped and grinned. 'Now you're not going to show me your muscles, are you, Charlie?' He put his hands on his hips, then frowned.

Gannon said, 'Every now and then you forget who's boss, Ben. Get down off your horse. It's lesson time.'

Clayton grinned. 'You want to fight me to prove I've been a bad boy, or to convince yourself you can still handle me?' He stepped from the saddle. 'I'm my own man, Charlie. If I lick you this time, we're through.'

'No, you won't be. Because you'll still need me. Come to me, Ben.'

He was awful quick, Gannon discovered;

Clayton's fist struck him under the heart and drove a white flame through him, right to the bowels, and he grappled until his mind stopped all that wheeling about.

He managed to hit Clayton and drive him back, then he caught a fist in the face, and gave Ben one back. To his surprise, Ben went down, but got up immediately, and they stood there, slugging each other. Only Gannon couldn't take that any more and he fell back as a blow exploded along side his head. The ground came up harder than he expected it to and he was stunned. In his mind, he kept saying to himself, 'You've got to get up, Charlie. Just this one more time. Get up and show him how good a man you are. Make him believe it.'

He found strength somewhere, and made it to his feet, then he went in for the one last time, the one final effort to get Ben Clayton, to show him that Charlie Gannon was the best still. And he got Ben good, flush on the jaw, another in the stomach, and a final punch, calling up all the strength in him. Clayton stretched flat on the sand.

It felt good to win, to know that there was that much left in him; he hadn't known, though, how close it would be. But he could keep it from Ben. Gannon was almost too weak, too winded to stand, but he forced himself and forced out the words, at the same time praying that Ben wouldn't call his bluff. 'Get up, Ben! I'm not finished!'

But he was finished and he knew it, and Ben just stayed where he was, shaking his head, trying to clear it. Then he sat up, and looked at Gannon; his smile was slow in building because his jaw ached, but he had been washed clean somehow. The resentment, the anger was gone.

He held up his hand for Gannon to give him a pull, and when he stood up, he said, 'Yes, boss?'

'Let's hope this is the last time,' Gannon said.

Clayton continued to grin and rub his jaw. 'You've got a punch like a mule kick, Charlie. I didn't think you had it in you.' Then he turned to his horse and mounted. 'Let's get to work, huh?'

CHAPTER SIX

Setting up a permanent camp took two days. With winter coming they would need a good shelter and probably wouldn't have the time later to erect it. They pitched three tents, the largest as a shelter for their saddle horses. The two smaller ones were used as a storage place and quarters.

Around each tent they piled rocks, sorting for pieces that fit, and ended up with a wall four feet high which would act as a snow break and keep the winds of winter from tearing the tents to pieces.

With this done, they selected a canyon-like fissure in one of the buttes for their horse trap, for the more natural the enclosure the less suspicious the horses would be when driven toward it. In selecting their canyon trap both men spent a day looking it over carefully to make sure there was only one way in and one way out. It would take them a week or ten days to find a herd and run them out enough to where they could be trapped, and they didn't want this work spoiled due to some escape path they hadn't seen.

It was important for them not to work afoot any more than could be helped; wild horses were smart and canny, and the slightest hint of something wrong could nullify their labor.

Their biggest job was the construction of the 'booger' wings, the wide, funnel-shaped openings necessary to guide the driven horses into the canyon and keep them from breaking away. With more men to work the herd, Gannon and Clayton would not have had to build such elaborate traps. But they had no help, so there was the job of pole setting to do, and they had to strip the area around their seep of small saplings, drag them three miles, and set them deep into the ground. Brush and foliage tied to the poles disguised them enough to fool the horses, then they strung the heavy strand wire. They built their booger wings

88

nearly seven hundred yards out from the trap entrance, a man-made funnel which, once entered, allowed no turning away. The mouth of the wings was wide spread, and they ripped up a blanket and tied bits of cloth to the wire. These would stir in the breeze and booger any horse that ran toward the fence.

All this work left them so tired at night that they could only eat and roll into their blankets, but it was good work, and when it was finally done, they knew they wouldn't have to do it over. While all this was going on, they had been grain-feeding their horses, saving them for the run. Actually they needed more saddle horses, but they only had five, counting the two Clayton had, now relieved of harness duty. Both men wondered if five horses could endure a run which might last three to four days. Trapping wild horses was not a matter of waving your slicker and pushing them into the trap. A wild horse, first contacting man, was as fast as a deer, with a stamina that bordered on the unbelievable. To catch them, a rider had to circle a herd, spook them into a wild run, and head them toward his partner, hiding down-country four or five miles. And just when your horse was ready to drop in his tracks, your partner would whoop it up, and try to drive them back. You had a chance then to change horses, and take over when the time came. A good run might cover from forty to sixty miles in one day. Then you night-camped and did it all over again, maybe for three or four days running. These were the things constantly going through Gannon's mind, and the plaguing wonder if they'd be able to do it. You just had to wear wild horses down before they'd go into a trap, and be fit to handle when they got there.

Ben Clayton won the toss, and he spent hours easing around behind the medium-sized herd they'd spotted while Gannon hunkered down to wait for the run to begin. It was, he knew, a killing time for a man and his horse. With a big herd, using ten or fifteen men, you could wear out three saddle horses a day, and by the time the run was over you were all but ruined yourself, too sore to sit, and too beat to stand.

Finally he saw the dust cloud, and put his ear to the ground to listen to the thunder there, then it was time for him to mount up, to take over, and there wasn't much time to think after that. It was a long day, full of sweat and choking dust, and a beginning pain in the small of his back that never used to be there at all. That night, he just drank some coffee and rolled up in his blankets, and the next morning, getting up was a hard thing.

This day was worse than the one before; in all he supposed they'd driven the herd some fourteen miles, direction-wise, but somewhere near a hundred, round-about-wise. Before the day was over, he knew he'd be bleeding again, and sure enough he was, when he made a brief stop. When darkness fell, they camped where they halted, ate cold, slept colder, and were mounted up before dawn. Changing horses wasn't much help now; the animals were tired and would need a week on grain just to pick up their tone.

A glance was all they needed between them to know that this was the last day of the run. Ready or not, the herd had to go into the trap, or be forgotten; there just wasn't another day's run in either man.

The herd was really bigger than two men could handle, thirty some horses, but they drove them on that last dead-heat run toward the trap, and pushed them in without losing a one. They didn't know how to speak of their relief, and worked hard to erect the high pole and wire barrier across the canyon's mouth.

They'd give the herd two or three days to simmer down now, get used to being boxed up. Aside from seeing that they had a little water, they could take it easy and hope some of the aches and pains would go away.

Ben Clayton fixed up a fire and cooked the first real meal they'd eaten in days. Charlie Gannon lay on his blankets, smoking. Ben was saying, 'That's not bad for the first trap, Charlie. I'd have been satisfied with fifteen or twenty.'

'I saw a colt in there I want to cut out and gentle a bit,' Gannon said. 'And there was a pinto that looks good for saddle work. We can use some spare horses.'

Ben frowned slightly. 'Well, I didn't figure to spend the time gentlin',' he said. 'It ain't going to be long until the first snow, and I was hoping we'd take down the booger wires and rig another trap. We can hold this herd in the canyon for a month anyway.'

'We've got to have a remuda,' Gannon said. 'You take that pinto and I'll cut out a couple more. In ten days we ought to start riding them.' He snubbed out his smoke. 'I'll gentle the colt myself.'

'For that kid?' Ben shook his head and smiled. 'Charlie, he really didn't take your promise seriously. Kids learn fast about grownups.'

This half angered Gannon, and he looked harshly at Ben Clayton. 'Yeah, maybe that's so, but I meant what I said. Now I don't want to talk about it any more.'

*　　　*　　　*

Harry Graves had to admit that Joe Kerry did know his part of the country like the back of his hand, and Graves guessed they'd covered it all, but without finding any trace of Gannon or Ben Clayton. The two horse wranglers had simply disappeared. Graves could see that this failure bothered Joe Kerry a good deal, for it put the man back on his own word, and made it the third time he'd come out second best; this bothered him the most.

For nearly twenty-five days now Graves had been studying his companions, and he enjoyed varying degrees of success. The brothers, Al and George, he catalogued easily; they were clan people, confining their talk to themselves and presenting to everyone else a silent semi-hostility. Graves had met their kind before and got along with them by simply leaving them alone.

Joe Kerry was different, more complex. He never talked about his past, but Graves could put it together pretty well for himself. Texas born and bred, with everything coming hard and no second chance at anything. Out of this came an early, simple philosophy: step on the other man before he steps on you; lie if it'll do the job better than the truth; and try to steal before you make an offer to buy.

There wasn't, Graves had to admit, such a broad area of difference between himself and Kerry, only Graves felt that his own background led to a refinement of these axioms which made them more socially acceptable since they became less obvious. In his own mind Graves felt more like an astute businessman or a shrewd banker, where the words cheat, lie, and steal had a shoddiness, yet application was quite workable. And thinking back about Gannon, Graves had to admit that being caught made him angrier than being called a crook.

Kerry broke into his thoughts when he said, 'Al, build a fire on that ridge over there and send up some smoke.'

They were just settling down to a night camp; it was not quite dark and they were in high ground. George started to build the cook fire up, and Graves just sat there, figuring that if Kerry wanted to explain himself, he would.

Kerry lit a cigar and stood there, puffing it, letting the firelight highlight his face. Then he said, 'If anyone knows where they are, the Indians will.' He rubbed the whiskers on his cheeks. 'The way I figure it, they've swung the Indians over to their side somehow. That's why we ain't seen hide nor hair of 'em since we've been here. Well, we'll soon know. They'll see the smoke and find our fire. One jug of whiskey ought to buy what I want to know.'

'You ought to have thought of that two weeks ago,' Graves said. 'This ground's getting harder every night.'

'It won't be long now,' Kerry said, hunkering down. 'And once I get this settled I'm going to put together a big outfit and go over into the Utah monument country in the spring. And this time I'm not going to be run out.'

Harry Graves frowned. 'I thought we were there now.'

'Naw,' Kerry said, laughing. 'That's way to hell and gone west of here. Another four or five days' ride.'

'Why, you stupid jackass, that's where Gannon and Clayton are now!' Graves snapped. 'You've wasted my time.'

'Don't talk that way to me,' Kerry warned. 'What's this about the monument country? How do you know?'

'Because they talked about it in Lordsburg,' Graves snapped. He got up and dusted off the seat of his pants. 'Friend, you just point the direction out to me, and I'll say good-bye.'

'Sit down,' Kerry said. 'You started with me, and you'll finish with me.' He gave Graves a little shove backwards. 'Don't rile me, mister; I'm in no mood for it now.' He raised his voice to Al up on the ridge. 'Make a lot of smoke there!' He was impatient and angry at himself and at Graves for pointing up his mistake. Kerry chewed on his cigar. 'It don't seem possible, but I guess it is. Somehow they won the Mormon woman over. She's big medicine with the Piutes and that old bag-of-bones chief they got.'

'How did you try to get on her good side? Offer her a drink of whiskey?'

'Say, you've got a smart mouth,' Kerry pointed out.

'And about six times as much brains as you have,' Graves said. He saw the quick anger come to Joe Kerry's eyes and held up his hands. 'Now you take one poke at me, mister, and you can go to hell. You want to get into that country without a good fight with the

Indians, then listen to me.'

'All right, but say the right things.'

'You've got all the drawing-room charm of a side-winder,' Graves said.

'That ain't the right thing,' Kerry warned.

'Shut up and listen. I knew Gannon and Clayton; they've got a kind of charm. Clayton's young and good-looking and women like him, and Gannon's the kind they like to mother. You, a woman would take a stick to.' He grinned at Kerry. 'Now I don't do bad with women. Not bad at all. So you have your little confab tonight with the Indians and talk them into guiding me into the monument country. Give me ten days, and I'll have the Mormon woman washing my shirts.'

Kerry frowned. 'Where does that leave me?'

'Better off than you are now,' Graves said. 'You ought to be able to get some whiskey into the chief's belly somehow.'

'I'd have to send it along with you,' Kerry said. 'Can't trust Indians. They'd have it drunk up before they got there.'

'All right, I'll take it. And I'll get a clean bill of health with the Mormon woman and her Indian friends. Then I'll find Clayton and Gannon, meet you ten days from now, and we'll be in and out with the job done before they know about it.'

'I like it,' Kerry said.

'Well, I thought you would,' Graves said. 'It's real sneaky.'

96

Kerry surprised him by not getting angry. He flung an arm around Harry Graves' shoulder and offered him one of his foul cigars. Then they sat by the fire and waited for the Indians to arrive.

*   *   *

The two wranglers built a small round holding corral of pole and wire with a stout snubbing pole in the center. Just the right size to break horses. There was no dispute between them as to who was going to do the cutting out, for Gannon was a wizard with a rope. While Clayton rode slowly among the captive herd, moving them, opening them up a little, Gannon set himself to make his cast. He took the colt first, busting him neatly by roping his two front feet, and throwing him. Then with Clayton's help, he tied him down with short hobbles and then worked him into the round breaking corral.

Gannon liked to work with a young horse; they were full of spirit, but they learned quickly. His first task was to slicker break the colt, and to play it safe, he always tied the animal down to do this. Never making a sudden move, he kept wiping his slicker gently over the animal until the fright left his eyes and he stopped quivering. A day or two of this, and he changed to a blanket, then later, his hands, all the time talking softly, soothingly, and by

97

the end of the week, the pony would lead, and stand still for a saddle blanket and saddle on his back.

Of course he was too young for a man to sit, yet each day Gannon found time to saddle the pony and lead him about, and even to place a sixty-pound bag of grain in the saddle to get the pony used to a boy's weight.

He had to work with Ben, breaking other horses. They worked the pinto and two roans, fine animals, full of old nick and bone-breaking knocks if a man wasn't careful.

Time was needed to turn a wild horse into any semblance of a work horse, and they didn't have that much time. Already there was a hint of frost in the morning air, and the nights, as soon as the sun dropped, turned chilly. A big fire was always welcome. These were the times when they talked about their catch, and about the ones they hadn't caught yet.

'The first snow's going to help us,' Ben Clayton said. 'I'd say north of here we'll find all the mustangs we can take.'

'Want to try using this trap over again?' Gannon asked. He had a cup of strong, hot coffee to his mouth and his words were muffled.

Clayton gave it some thought. 'Well, we ain't faunched around the booger any. By the time they got wind that it was a trap, it'd be too late for 'em to turn out.'

'That was my notion,' Charlie Gannon said.

'We'll use it again next week. The herd that's in the canyon is used to it now, and will make good bait. I'll chance it rather than spend another ten days building a new one.'

'We'll have to tear the booger out if we do; we're about out of wire.'

'It's settled then,' he said and got up. He had a tin pail of water heating and now took this off the fire. From his saddlebag he produced soap and a razor and a small polished tin mirror.

'You goin' somewhere?' Ben asked.

Gannon stripped to the skin and began to bathe, shivering all the while. 'I thought I'd ride over to see Mrs. Regan,' he said, matter-of-factly. 'I'll be back by mornin'.' He tacked this last on as though he expected to hear a strong objection.

Ben said, 'Four miles to the trap from camp, and four miles back, and horse breakin' all day; ain't that enough to keep you busy, Charlie?'

Gannon towelled himself dry with a thin blanket. 'What's the matter, Ben? The old vinegar gone?'

'I'll be going when you're sitting,' Clayton said quickly. 'It just don't make sense to me, you riding all the way over there. Hell, it'll be nine or ten o'clock when you get there. Time for a decent—well, never mind. It ain't my business.'

'The truth if I ever heard it,' Gannon said and put on his underwear. He hunched down

99

to soak his face and shave, and when he was finished he put the razor and soap away.

'You going to take the kid's pony?' Clayton asked.

Gannon shook his head. 'Not yet. I want to gentle him some more. I don't want him to get thrown and hurt.'

'He's bound to get thrown,' Clayton said. 'Charlie, we can't afford to fool around with that pony.'

'I'll decide that,' Gannon said.

He shook the dust from his clothes the best he could, and dampened a rag and cleaned the black hat; he was very careful of it, as though it had cost him the last hundred dollars to his name.

'Don't wait up for me,' he said and got his horse and rode out.

Ben Clayton drank another cup of coffee, then gathered his blankets, a lantern and his rifle, and got ready to leave. This was his turn at night guard, sleeping with the herd, and they alternated every night. It was a cold, lonely job, full of noises and darkness and jerking wide awake a dozen times, and always finding it hard to go back to sleep because you never really did find out what woke you in the first place.

After putting out the fire, he saddled up and rode over to the trap and took his station high in the rocks, on a small ledge that gave him a commanding sweep of the herd. Or what

100

would have been a commanding sweep if there'd been any light at all.

Clayton always figured this night guard to be some silliness thought up by a cranky boss with too many men on his hands, for he sure couldn't see what he could do if a cat got in there, as they often did. It just meant a lot of noise and a dead animal, with the cat getting clean away. But the night guard was part of the duty, and because Gannon did it without complaint Ben Clayton sure wasn't going to object and give Gannon any chance to say that he was a griper.

Alone with his own thoughts, Ben had to admit that he was always sorely put to keep ahead of Gannon, and most of the time he just could manage to keep up with him. He had horse savvy and man savvy, and the kind of guts that didn't know when to quit or admit they were licked. Like during the run. By golly, there had been times when Ben thought he'd just keel over in the saddle. He'd passed blood too, but had kept it to himself, because he was sure the pounding hadn't bothered Gannon, and Ben just couldn't bear to have Gannon think bad of him.

Thinking back, Ben recalled the early years they'd been together, when he hadn't been any more than a gangling towhead with big feet and sometimes a big mouth. Now and then that nearly got him in serious trouble, but somehow just being with Gannon made it pass.

He had never known that he could admire a man more than he admired Gannon, and yet feel pushed apart from him, driven there by a sense of competition he couldn't control. All he knew was that he had to be good because Gannon was good, and no matter how good Gannon got, Ben Clayton would have to be better.

If he didn't do that, he knew that Gannon would soon stop liking him.

The night was cold and his coat was none too warm, so Ben sat with the blanket around his shoulders, and later he put it over his head like a small tent. He wished he could build a fire. Actually there was nothing stopping him except that Charlie had said some weeks before that they ought to conserve wood, and since Gannon sat out his guard tour in the cold, Ben Clayton did the same.

He fell asleep after a while, but woke up with a start, trying to sort out the noise that penetrated his mind so sharply. After listening for a moment, he decided that it was nothing.

Then he felt the hair on his neck rise and threw off the blanket and grabbed his rifle and knocked over his lantern, all at the same time, as the silence was pierced by a mountain lion's scream. He knew what it meant, and groped for matches to light the lantern. A horse was down, screaming, and the herd was smashing about in panic.

It was worth his life to leave his place and

enter the trap, but he had to. Swinging the lantern, he threw it and watched the bright arc of it and the shatter of it, then the wide flare of ignited coal oil. It cast a dancing light and he saw the horse down, and the cat. Whipping up his rifle, he fired, too soon, too quickly, and the bullet struck behind the cat.

This was enough, though, and with a leap and a bound he was gone, leaving the dead horse behind. Hurrying down off his perch, Ben entered the canyon and began to scrape together dried brush and made a big pile of it and set it afire.

There was a horse screaming in the rocks, and he went to investigate; a mare was down with a shattered foreleg. Fright had driven her to a panicked charge right into the rocks, where she had stumbled and fallen.

It always hurt Ben deep in his heart to shoot a horse, still he had to do it. Levering in another shell, he put the muzzle near the mare's head and ended her misery.

The fact that he was in the trap caused the herd to bunch at one end; man was an enemy, but not in the same category as a cat. Then he turned and went back to see to the downed horse.

He could see the animal better now that the brush pile was blazing high, and he stared for a moment, then said, 'Aw, no! God damn it, no!'

The pony was dead, his throat torn, a bright puddle of blood still spreading on the ground.

Ben thought of all the times he'd cussed that pony because of Gannon and his time-consuming patience in gentling the animal. Now he was sorry he'd even thought those things, because he was jealous that Gannon had thought of offering the pony and not him.

Ben walked over and sat down on a small rock, shook out his sack of tobacco and started to make a cigaret. He formed the paper, licked it, and put a match to it, then inhaled deeply to get a good bite of it.

He wondered what he'd say to Charlie Gannon in the morning, how he'd tell him that a damned cat had gotten in and killed the pony. Probably right now Gannon was getting Beans out of bed and telling him all about the pony, and the boy's eyes would be round with the wonder and delight of it, and here the damned pony was, lying in its own blood puddle.

Ben thought of all the promises that had been made to him as a kid, all of them that had come to nothing, and all the tears he'd shed. Then he'd grown to an age where it was proper to hide the hurt, pretend it didn't matter, but it would always matter.

He threw his cigaret away and walked around in a choppy circle feeling all the anger come back, all the stored up hurt, and in a way it was so big he couldn't bear to carry it all. So he said, 'Aw, Charlie, damn it, what did you go off and leave me for?' He felt loneliness close in like hands touching him, and he didn't think he could stand it any longer, this acute sense of desertion. So he raised his voice and bounced his cry off the mute walls.

'Charlie! Charlie, come back!'

He listened to the echoes fade and wished that somehow he'd have stood up to Gannon and gone with him. It just wasn't good, Gannon going off and leaving him this way because no matter how he tried he just couldn't rid himself of the notion that sometime, someday, he wouldn't come back.

CHAPTER SEVEN

The lights of Jenny Regan's place were a beacon guiding Gannon those last miles, and as he drew near the yard he saw her come from the small barn, a lantern in one hand and a bucket in the other. When she heard his horse approaching, she stopped and stood still, not afraid, just waiting for whoever it was to get close enough to be identified. He dismounted at the perimeter of the lantern light, and she held it up, so that it shone more directly on him.

'Why, what a nice surprise,' she said.

He took the pail, containing milk, and followed her to the house, talking all the way. 'I suppose I shouldn't have dropped in like this, but I was out this way and I thought—'

She stopped in the doorway and smiled. 'Now, Charlie, you know you rode over here just to see me.' A slight, pleased blush came to her cheeks. 'And if you didn't, let me think so.'

'The fact is, I did come to see you,' Gannon said. He laughed with relief. 'It was a bold thing, I guess.'

'It was a good thing, Charlie Gannon. A very good thing.'

He strained the milk for her and lowered it into a small cistern she had, and by the time he was done she had some coffee made and had put out a plate of cookies.

'I expect the boy's asleep,' Gannon said. He glanced briefly at her. 'In the morning, tell him I caught a pony for him.'

Jenny drew her breath in sharply and clapped her hands together. 'Oh, what a wonderful thing to do,' she said. 'You have no idea how much he's wanted one.' She folded her hands together and looked at them, then spoke more softly. 'I prayed that you meant the words you spoke to him, Charlie. I wanted them to be true, for him, and for me.'

'How for you?' he asked.

From her expression he supposed it was a question he shouldn't have asked, for it was one she was probably not ready to answer. Yet she said, 'I wanted you to be a man who never spoke lightly of a thing, Charlie. To a child, or a woman.'

106

'I wouldn't,' he assured her. Then he smiled and switched the subject. 'You make good coffee, Jenny.'

'My Adam used to say that the day didn't really start until he'd had a cup of my coffee. You don't mind my talking about him, do you?'

'No,' he said. 'The man was a part of your life, Jenny.'

'Yes, he was. A serene man, my Adam. Once I thought he was too old for me; he was over forty when he died. The first time I ever saw him was at a trading market, and he picked up a baby chick and it wasn't afraid to be in his hands. I knew then that we'd be happy.'

'Was he picked for you?' Gannon asked.

'No, but the elders wanted Adam to have a wife and me to have a husband. I learned to love him, Charlie. That's the truth.' She regarded him seriously for a time. 'Did you mind my saying that?'

He shook his head. 'I'm not jealous of the man, Jenny, or that he made you smile.' He finished what was left of his coffee before asking what was on his mind. 'Ain't it so that Mormons have more than one wife?'

'Some have had more than one,' she said. 'Adam didn't hold to it. Neither do I.' Then she tipped her head back and laughed happily. 'But Adam is dead, Charlie, and we're not. It's good to remember without hurt, but there are other things too. Did you catch many horses?'

'Oh, a fair herd,' he said. 'Ben and I want to

107

trap another bunch before the snow comes. And that ain't far off.' He reached for his tobacco, then thought better of it.

She said, 'You can smoke.'

He rolled a cigaret and took his light from the lamp. 'With just two of us, it's hard to work a herd that's a proper size. Well, we'll make out the best we can. In spring I'd like to have sixty anyway that were halter broke.'

'The Indians would help you,' Jenny said. 'Why don't you ask Shanti? His people are camped no more than twenty-five miles from here. If you gave them a few horses, or some trade goods—'

'We didn't bring much to trade,' Gannon said. 'But we'd give them horses. Where we need the help is during the run.' He explained how wild horses were hunted, how you had to keep them away from water for a few days and run them ragged so they'd be too tired to fight once they got into the trap.

'Shanti would give you men,' she said. 'In past years he's helped the Mormons who came here for horses.' She snapped her fingers. 'Charlie, why don't I ride to Shanti's camp tomorrow and speak for you? You could stay here and mind the stock and Beans; I'd be back the day after tomorrow.'

'Ben's expecting me back.'

'But you'll save so much time,' she pointed out. 'Charlie, it won't be long until the snow flies, and if you can make one more big catch you won't have to bother with that again. All winter long you can stay in camp and gentle the horses for the spring drive.'

What she said made a lot of sense; it *was* the way to do it, no two ways about that. 'All right,' Charlie Gannon said. 'But I sure hate to think of you riding all that way alone.'

'Nothing's going to hurt me,' she said and touched his hand. 'You worry too much about other people, Charlie.'

'Only the ones I like,' Gannon said. When she started to take her hand off his, he quickly reached out and held it there. 'I like your touch, Jenny. Don't take it away from me.'

Her hand remained still, and she looked at him steadily, the lamplight accenting the strong bones of her face. Her lips were full and soft and curving in that half smile she always wore when she had to be serious, yet not hard.

'The only things we have to fear out here is ourselves, Charlie. I don't need a year of soft light and roses and buggy rides to know a man, and it would be the easiest thing in the world for me to tell you to stay, that Beans needs a man. That I need a man.' She withdrew her hand gently. 'We have to be very careful, Charlie. Do you know?'

He blew out a full, deep breath, and rolled another cigaret. Then he said, 'I'm a man who's always been alone, and a few hours with you has made me dissatisfied with it. It's been foolish of me to have thought the things I've thought; you need more of a man than I am.'

This puzzled her and she said, 'What do you mean?'

He pushed back his chair and got up. 'I'm a horse wrangler. That's not much.'

Her frown remained, lining her forehead; she continued to watch him. He said, 'Your husband was a man who could build with his hands and he was good with the boy, and with you. I don't know if I'm any of those things. I don't even know if I'd want to live your life here, or have you live mine with me.' He reached out and picked up his hat. 'It's late.'

'You can sleep here by the fire,' Jenny said evenly.

He hesitated, then shook his head. 'I'll find some hay in the barn. And you won't have to worry none about me comin' inside before I hear you up and about.'

'I know that,' she said. Then her smile came again, quick and bright, making her face vibrantly alive. 'Charlie, put on the hat.'

'What?' he said, then settled it on his head.

'It looks nice, Charlie. Real nice.'

* * *

Ben Clayton's anger really didn't come to a boil until midday, then he just threw everything down, caught up his horse, and rode toward Jenny Regan's place to have it out with her and Charlie Gannon.

110

By God, if Gannon wanted to up and leave, to wipe out all the friendship of five years standing, he could at least be man enough to do it to his face.

Approaching the Regan place, Ben realized that he hadn't really noticed it before; it was a good little farm. Wooden troughs fed water from the spring to a large watering tank, which in turn irrigated a small garden patch, some pasture, and took care of the stock.

And it deeply insulted him to see Charlie Gannon in that garden, a hoe in hand, cleaning it up like some paid farm worker. Beans was there with a big basket, dragging the dead residue to a pile where it was being burned.

As Clayton rode up, Gannon looked around, then took out his handkerchief and wiped sweat from his forehead. 'Hello there, Ben. There's a rake in the barn, if you feel ambitious.'

Clayton didn't say anything. He just walked over and knocked Charlie Gannon down. On the ground, Gannon shook his head, then looked up at Ben Clayton. He said, 'I'm goin' to sit here until you tell me why, and if the reason ain't good enough, I'm goin' to get up and give it to you good.'

'That's for goin' off and leaving me,' Clayton said flatly. '*I'd* have said good-bye, at least.' He turned his head and looked around. Beans was standing by the fire, looking solemn and a little worried. 'Where's the woman, Charlie?'

111

'Do you mean, Jenny?'

'Yeah, I mean Jenny!'

'She's gone to Shanti's village to fetch some Piutes back with her,' Gannon said. 'They're going to help us on the next mustang run.'

It was a hard thing for Ben Clayton to take this, but he knew Gannon would not lie to him, which put all the mistake on Clayton—the false presumption, the unwarranted anger, the error in judgment that led him to hit Gannon in the first place.

'Well,' he said, trying to save something out of this, 'you could have told me.'

'We decided last night, Ben,' Gannon said. He got up slowly and dusted off his pants. Stepping close to Clayton, he said, 'I swear, Ben, there's times when I think you're a damned kid who can't let go of the coat tail. I said I'd be back, didn't I? Well, damn it, believe me. And what difference does it make if I'm a day or two late?' He picked up his hoe with a savage sweep. 'Now get the shovel and give me a hand here.'

'All right,' Clayton said, sounding very deflated. Then he took Gannon by the arm and spoke softly so the boy wouldn't hear. 'I hate to say it, but the pony's dead. A cat got in. I had to shoot a mare who broke her leg.'

Gannon couldn't help looking at the boy before he spoke. 'Don't mention it again, to him or to Jenny. I'll just have to get the boy another pony, that's all.'

'Charlie, by the time we're through with another run, the snow'll be here.'

'Damn it, I can't help that!' he snapped.

'I'm sorry,' Clayton said sincerely. 'You believe me, Charlie?'

'Why should I blame you?' Gannon said. 'Nobody likes a cat in with a herd, and there's no way I know of to keep 'em out. What did you do with the dead horses?'

'Dragged 'em out,' Ben said. 'If we could spare the time, we ought to hunt that cat before he comes back.'

'We'll see,' Gannon said softly and began hoeing again. While Clayton was getting the shovel, Gannon thought this whole thing over, deciding that one of them ought to go back to their camp and keep an eye on the horse herd. With the cat making one kill, there was a strong likelihood that he'd come back. When Ben came back, Gannon put his hoe down and said, 'You stay here until Jenny gets back. I'll go watch the horses.'

'You made your deal with her,' Clayton said. 'I'll go.'

'Already made up my mind,' Gannon said. 'Just take care of the boy and feed him proper. You tell Jenny that I had to go back, huh?' He said it as though he was tired of arguing and wanted it settled once and for all.

'All right,' Ben said. 'Charlie, you ain't stuck on her, are you? That ain't why you came over here, is it? I mean, you just wanted to tell her

113

and the boy about the pony, didn't you?'

Gannon opened his mouth and almost said that he went because he couldn't get her out of his mind, because she'd struck a responsive chord deep within him that called up to his mind all the things he had done without in his life, the things that hadn't been important before but were important now.

But looking at Ben Clayton he knew he wouldn't say any of these things. And he wouldn't say anything in denial either. 'I'll get on back,' he said, and went over to talk to Beans.

Ben felt as though a door had been slammed in his face, a door so big and heavy that he would never be able to beat it down. Gannon said something to the boy, then put his arms around him briefly and went to the barn for his horse.

He rode out a moment later, raising a pall of dust.

Beans came over and pulled at Ben Clayton's chaps. 'Mum's got cookies. Can I have some?'

'Huh? Oh, sure, kid. Sure.'

The boy ran to the house and Ben Clayton picked up the hoe. It sure didn't take much to make a child happy, he saw. Maybe a few cookies, or a pony. His thinking darkened then. By golly, *he'd* get the pony this time. Not to steal any thunder away from Gannon, but just because he'd feel a lot better about it.

114

It left him feeling kind of pecked, the way Gannon took off, almost as soon as he arrived. It seemed to Ben that Gannon was not very eager to have anything to do with him. Of course, Gannon's reasons for going back were sound enough, but Ben still couldn't get it clear of his mind that Jenny Regan had something to do with this.

He hadn't thought her particularly pretty. Oh, she was, he guessed, but she was *old*, hell, nearly thirty anyway. She still had her shape and all that, and a way of smiling that made a man want to jump right up and do what she asked.

Well, that might work on Charlie Gannon, but he'd be danged if it would work on him.

And he held that thought closely, sort of a protective garment, until Jenny Regan returned.

When she saw that Gannon was gone and that Ben had taken his place, no sign of disappointment crossed her face. She shook hands with Ben and the boy put up her horse, then the two of them went into the house. She took off the scarf she had tied around her hair, and shook the dust from it.

'Shanti will send four men. They'll be at your camp sometime tomorrow,' she said.

'That's nice,' Clayton said. 'But I guess Charlie and I would have got along all right.'

'Why, of course you would,' she said. 'Only now you'll get along better.' She poured a pan of water at the wash table, unbuttoned the front of her dress part way, and tucked the collar in away from her neck and shoulders. 'This dust in my hair has been itching all the way home.'

Clayton sat at the table and watched her wash her hair. Then he said, 'Ben stayed the night, huh?'

She raised her arm and looked under it without raising up from the wash basin. 'He slept in the barn, Ben. Don't go thinking the wrong things.'

'I won't,' he said. 'Charlie and I've been friends for a long time. No woman has come between us.'

'But you think I have?' She wrapped a towel around her head and straightened, turning so she could look at him.

'I sure think you're trying,' Clayton said, getting up. 'And I'll tell you something—don't!' He waved his hand toward the outside. 'I cleaned up your garden, straightened up the barn, and put new hinges on the outhouse door because Charlie would have done it if he'd stayed. I did it because he wanted me to, not for you.'

'But I can thank you just the same, can't I?'

'It don't matter to me if you don't,' Clayton said. 'I want things to go on the way they've been going, Jenny. Sure, I guess it'll end sometime, but I'll end it; nobody will do it for me.'

She didn't seem angry at all with him, and this irritated him. Jenny Regan said, 'Ben, suppose you'd met a girl and liked her a lot. Who would come first? Her? Or Charlie Gannon?'

'Charlie would.'

She shook her head. 'I can see that you've yet to meet her. Ben, I wouldn't want to hurt you. I wouldn't steal something that's yours. But Charlie Gannon is his own man, whether you like it or not.' Her fingers refastened the buttons of her dress, and she made a turban of the towel. 'You were angry some time ago because I offered my help. It somehow hurt your manly pride, Ben. Can't you make up your mind what you want to do? You work so hard to be better than Charlie Gannon. It's in everything you do. You've got to go on showing him that you're as good or better. Then show him, Ben. When spring comes, shake his hand and tell him you might see him again sometime, and just ride off on your own.'

Clayton studied her while she talked, then he said, 'You can come right out with a thing when you get a notion to, can't you?'

'Sometimes I don't want to, Ben. Sometimes I have no choice.' Her smile was a faint curving of her lips. 'You want to hurt me, don't you? You want to put me in my place once and for all. All right, if it makes you feel better, go ahead. But try to remember that Charlie Gannon raised you, in a way. Don't make him

117

sorry he did it.'

'Boy, you just can't argue with a woman,' Clayton said, with some disgust. 'Well, I guess you got cards I'll never have, and you'll go right ahead and play 'em no matter what I say.' He turned to the door and stopped there. 'I'm going back. Maybe I won't see you again. Or Charlie either. Right now it don't seem like too good an idea to winter out here. Maybe we ought to take the horses we got and clear out.'

'Do you think you can talk him into doing that?'

'I talked him into coming here in the first place,' Ben Clayton said. He wanted to tell her about the pony; that would really hurt her, but he had a better way. 'Charlie needs me, Jenny. I've got to kind of hold him up all the time so he don't fall down. You or nobody else could take my place because he couldn't really cut a job any more without me.'

'That's not the truth,' she said. 'If it was, you wouldn't hang on five minutes, because you're young and you have no patience. Ben, when Charlie's so crippled he can't sit a horse, he'll be more man than you are. And you know it down in your soul.'

He wanted to laugh in her face, to tell her off good, but the words just wouldn't come up. Instead he wheeled and nearly knocked Beans down getting away from her. He caught up his horse, went into the saddle without touching a stirrup and rode out at much too fast a pace to

118

last.

Beans stood by his mother for a time, trying to be interested in the retreating man. Then he said, 'I ate all the cookies, Mum.'

'Well, we'll bake some more,' she said and turned him into the house.

*   *   *

Of all the drunk men Harry Graves had seen in his life, none of them had been Indians. He was amazed and a little horrified at what two full jugs did to Shanti's village. There wasn't a man there who wasn't all wobbly legs and holler, and he counted himself lucky that they hadn't yet come into the possession of firearms. They'd probably have shot each other, and him too, just for the fun of it.

The best thing he could do, he decided, was to get out, make a night camp away someplace and just sit tight for a few days until the hangover passed. Most white men were mean enough after a rip-roaring evening, and he suspected that the Piutes with their savage tendencies would be inclined to let blood, particularly his. There just was no sense of obligation in an Indian's make-up.

No one saw Harry Graves leave; he could be very quiet when he wanted to. Shanti was sitting on his blanket, singing all the old songs with all the vocal volume of the intoxicated. And the singing made him remember, made

119

him sad, for he thought about his little Tonsha, long dead now, just a handful of bones sewn into a small bag.

The tragedy was so real to Shanti, so sharp, that he felt he had to change it or die from the pain in his old heart. The white man's sickness had taken the boy in the bloom of youth, and although Shanti had never thought much about it before, he felt it entirely just to take a white child in return.

He staggered erect, called some braves about him, and quickly told them of his grief. A vision had come to him, he claimed, and the spirits had talked with him, showed him the way, and who could argue with a chief who has talked with spirits?

A gathering of the horses, a final burst of shouting, and they dashed away. Two braves fell off their horses and were not missed, for the blood was up in them and they would have attacked a column of General Crook's cavalry had it been handy.

Through the night and across the desert floor they stormed, and each leap of the horse only heightened their resolve to follow their beloved chief.

Jenny Regan was wakened by the muted throb of their running horses and she barely had time to get out of bed, slip into her chemise and light the lamp before they came into the yard. Quickly throwing a blanket around her, she opened the door and saw them dismounting, or falling off their horses; it was difficult to tell.

They staggered up to her, and Shanti thrust out his old arm like a stick of oak and knocked her partially back into the room. She saw their eyes then, and smelled the whiskey on them.

Still no real fear came to her. 'Where did you get whiskey?' she demanded, standing her ground.

They whooped and one of them did a dance around her kitchen. Shanti grinned toothlessly and said, 'Whiskey good!'

'You get out of here,' Jenny said. 'And don't you come back until you're sober!'

Beans, disturbed by it all, poked his head out of the back room to see what all the commotion was about. Shanti saw him, held out his arms. 'Boy! Me take!'

'You leave him alone,' Jenny said, moving in front of him, blocking his way. 'Beans, lock the door!'

'Him mine!' Shanti insisted.

He grabbed her and tried to push her aside, and she pushed back at him. Her blanket fell during the struggle and one of the Indians grabbed the back of her chemise and ripped it clear to her waist. She was a modest woman, but it had no place in her thinking now. With the torn chemise falling down her waist, she grabbed the old chief around the neck and tried to wrestle him to the floor.

Beans, frightened now, slammed his door

121

and shot the bolt, and Shanti lost his gentleness. He struck her with his fist, got her away from him, then reached for the milk crock sitting on the table.

Jenny was on one knee, trying to get up, when he fractured it across the crown of her head. For a moment she hung there, as though some strength not her own was holding her up, then she fell forward on her face and the split in her scalp started to ooze blood onto the floor.

They had no trouble breaking down the boy's door; two Indians battered it with all the furniture they could get their hands on, and finally the lock gave.

They dragged the crying boy out, and Shanti kicked his braves to make them stop being rough. He put his skinny arms around the struggling boy and said, 'You mine! Huh?'

Then he picked him up and they all went outside and got on their horses and rode away.

CHAPTER EIGHT

Ben Clayton always knew that Charlie Gannon was a great one for working up a worry, so when Gannon kept climbing up on the highest rocks for his look, Clayton didn't pay much attention.

The morning was wearing on, and there was

no sign of the Indians; Clayton supposed that was what was upsetting Gannon so much, that the day was being wasted. He got tired of being alone, so he climbed up to where Gannon sat. Gannon had his telescope in hand, and a sour expression on his face.

'Somehow it doesn't figure,' he said, not turning his head. 'I can't shake the feelin' that something's wrong.'

'Indians ain't reliable, Charlie,' Ben said. 'Let me see that telescope.' It was a battered instrument, not too powerful, and Ben extended its three sections and took a slow, scanning look at the desert and buttes. Then he snapped it shut. 'I don't see nothing.' His breath was frosty when he talked; a constant, piercing chill was in the air.

'Shanti wouldn't go back on his word to Jenny,' Gannon said. He took the telescope and again had a long, careful look. A gauze layer of clouds filtered the winter sun's light, and the desert seemed lifeless. Gannon swore softly and rolled a cigaret.

'Ain't somebody makin' smoke over there?' Ben Clayton asked.

'Where?' Gannon asked, and Ben pointed.

He put the telescope to his eye and swung it to take in a far cluster of buttes. Through the glass he could see clearly the rise of yellowish, thick smoke, and just knew without thinking that it wasn't made by any Indian.

'That's Jenny Regan's place!' he snapped,

123

jumping to his feet. He started to jump and slide off the rocks, working his way to the bottom of the draw where the horses were. Ben followed him, and by the time he got down Gannon was half saddled up.

'Ain't you jumpin' to conclusions, Charlie?'

Gannon didn't even glance at him; he pulled the cinch tight and went into the saddle. 'You stay here,' he said. 'If I ain't back by noon tomorrow, come looking for me.'

'I—' Ben closed his mouth because Gannon was already flogging his horse into a run. Ben watched him for a moment, then whipped off his hat and flung it on the ground; there just wasn't any way for a man to get around a tricky woman.

*　　　*　　　*

Jenny Regan's first impression was that she was terribly cold, and it was some time before she could understand why. A gray dawn light was growing slowly, and she lay on the floor, shivering, letting awareness come to her a fragment at a time. She was cold, she decided, because she had very few clothes on, and because she was sleeping on the floor without a blanket. If only her head didn't hurt so dreadfully, throbbed so insistently, she could think better. This was her conclusion.

When she tried to raise her head, she found that she could lift it only so far, then something clutched her hair and prevented her from raising further. It wasn't the pain, she was sure, and ran exploring hands along the floor until she found her long hair matted there as though imbedded in hardened honey.

The riddle of it held her still, and she lay there, breathing heavily, watching her breath turn into a pale fog. She was hurt somehow, and thought about it, let the pieces fall into their places, then she closed her eyes as though fighting back a siege of stomach sickness.

The Indians had come and taken the boy, and Shanti had hit her as they fought. She remembered it all now; why she was on the floor was no longer a mystery, and her hair was caught in her own dried blood.

Understanding helped her bear the pain; the side of her head felt like a tender boil, but large enough to spread the hurt into her eyes and jaw and down one side of her body.

There wasn't much strength in her, she knew, so she planned carefully, so as not to make a mistake and waste what was left of her. She was alone, and she needed help. How to get it caused her some concern. Then she worked out a plan as she lay there, went through it several times to sort out the flaws, and found none.

Getting her hair unstuck from the bare wood floor was not simple; she dared not take a deep breath and jerk free for fear of starting the bleeding of her scalp. So she freed her hair a bit at a time, grasping it, pulling it free without putting a strain on the roots.

Standing, she found, was impossible. As soon as she sat up she became so sick and dizzy that she promptly fell over on her back and lay there, staring at the ceiling. She was so cold; a dress, a blanket would have been a blessed relief, but she knew now how little strength she had and wouldn't waste it foolishly to cover herself.

Crawling, she got out of the house and onto the cold ground and, a foot at a time, sometimes mere inches at a time, she worked toward the barn and the watering trough. When she got to it, she found that it had a thin film of ice on it, too thick to break with her hands. What she planned was a big chance to take, but it had to be done; she needed a shock to her system to gather what strength she had left, summon it for one final, brief effort. Using her hands on the wooden sides of the trough, she pulled herself up, became sick, fought on in spite of it, then when she was balanced, half erect, she simply let herself topple forward into the tank. Her weight fractured the ice and she went under, a thousand shoots of shocking pain going through her, then she clawed and struggled and came up, her breath releasing explosively.

The immersion drove the pain from her head and she found that she could stand, even climb out of the trough. Her chemise hung in tatters, precariously perched on the round swell of her hips, and the cold dawn seemed even colder, more intense.

She went on to the barn, staggering to the door and pushing it open. Exactly how she got the stock out she wasn't sure, but when it was empty, she took down the lantern, lit it, then swung it, breaking it against a stanchion. The coal oil ignited and spread rapidly in the strewn hay, and the heat felt blessed good and she had to fight the impulse to just stay there and let it warm her.

With the last bit of her strength she ran from the barn and fell in the yard to roll over on her back. She turned her head and watched the fire build up, destroy the work of Adam Regan's hands, sending a spiral of thick yellow smoke up higher than the butte tops, a signal no man could miss within a radius of twenty miles.

Then she gave way to her weakness and lay there, her eyes closed, too tired to move, too tired to even care now.

She didn't want to open her eyes and watch the barn burn; it was bad enough to lie there and hear the flames consume the timbers, hear them fracture and collapse. Adam had worked so hard on that barn; it was built better than most men's homes, and she was burning the labor of his hands and heart to summon another man, a man who could make her forget Adam Regan. It seemed to be a twisted, ironic turn, but she felt that Adam Regan approved of it; he would have liked Charlie Gannon, for Regan too had known loneliness.

The barn took a long time to burn, for even after the rafter collapsed and the roof fell in, the pile of wreckage continued to burn, to shoot skyward a column of thick smoke.

And he would see it, she knew. He would see it because already his heart was turned toward her, and so followed a man's eyes. He'd see it and come to her and then it would be all right, for she found a comfort in him; he was a strong man. Some were like that, growing stronger in their minds and hearts while their exterior strength deteriorated.

Later she made her way back to the house, mostly on her hands and knees. The room was a shambles, furniture broken and dishes smashed; she wondered what made Indians smash things like that. She got into her bedroom and just sat on the floor until this wave of dizziness passed, then she pulled herself to the dresser and wash stand and dared a look in the mirror.

She did not recognize herself at all. One side of her face was swollen and blood-caked, and the five-inch split in her scalp made her ill when she looked at it; she would have sworn she could see the whiteness of bone there.

Still she set about washing her hair as best she could, washing the dirt off her body. It made her feel better somehow and she took off what was left of her chemise and managed to slip into a dress and crawl to the bed. After a rest on the floor, she pulled herself up and sank back; there was nothing to do now but wait.

Wait and try not to think of Beans.

*   *   *

Joe Kerry and the Manners brothers were camped high, near a hidden spring, and when Harry Graves got back he could not help but feel some disappointment, for they didn't seem particularly glad to see him.

There was some coffee on the fire, and he poured a cup before saying anything; to hell with them, he thought. It won't hurt them to wait a bit.

Finally Joe Kerry said, 'Well?'

Harry Graves looked around at him. 'Well what?'

'You know damned good and well what,' Kerry said. He raised a hand and rubbed his heavy face. 'All the whiskey gone?' Graves nodded briefly and Kerry grunted. 'Well, you took your time anyway.'

'Next time *you* take the whiskey to Shanti's village,' Graves suggested.

'Never mind getting smart. Did you soften up the Mormon woman yet?'

'I will,' Graves said. 'But first I'm going to eat, then shave. I don't want to look like you

129

when I knock on her door.'

Kerry's thin skin soaked up this insult and he pretended to pass it off, only Graves wasn't fooled much; the man was just filing it where he could recall it later. I'll probably have to shoot him, Graves thought, and began to fix a meal for himself.

It gave him a lot of pleasure to have the upper hand, even if it wasn't much; Graves hated to take orders from men like Joe Kerry, and if he played this right, he never would have to. Kerry was tough, but so was a mule, and that didn't make him smart.

While he cooked his meat, Graves said, 'Give me a day with the woman, then come on in.'

'You sound pretty sure of yourself,' Kerry said. 'Don't he, George?'

'Too sure,' George Manners said.

'Well!' Graves said, grinning. 'He speaks!'

'Joe, let me punch him in the face,' George begged.

'Later you can have him,' Kerry promised. 'You hear that, Graves? I just promised you to George.'

'In that case I don't think I'll go see the Mormon woman,' Graves said softly. 'Go hump it the hard way for all I care.' This was his top card and he played it with confidence, knowing that right now Joe Kerry needed him.

Kerry stood there for a moment, rubbing his unshaven chin. Then he said, 'Now if I call you,

I'm in for a tough time, ain't I? Still, them Indians got a sniff of whiskey, and they might do business if I promise 'em more. Maybe I can get by without the Mormon woman.' His glance switched to George Manners. 'You can have him now; he's no good to me.'

George was starting to rise when Harry Graves flipped the skillet full of meat and hot grease right in his face. With a howl of pain, George clapped both hands over his face and fell rolling on the ground. Without a moment of hesitation, Graves jumped to one side and when he faced Al Manners, he had a small .41 Derringer pointed at him, and pulled the trigger before Al even made a move toward his own gun. The two-shot popped like a misfire, and Al smashed his left hand at the sting on his breast. Slowly, blood seeped from between his fingers and he sat down, his face full of surprise and pain.

Joe Kerry didn't move; he was looking at the under barrel of the gun, and thinking about the live round left there. Harry Graves was most serious when he said, 'You made a mistake, Kerry. A real big one.'

Al was breathing heavily, and he said, 'Joe, help me. I'm hurt, Joe.'

'Help yourself,' Kerry said unkindly. 'I've got troubles of my own.' He did not take his attention off Harry Graves. 'What's this going to get you anyway?'

'A little nearer to a promise I made Gannon

and Clayton,' he said. 'Don't come after me, Kerry. I've still got you fixed good, because when I get to the Mormon woman's place, I'll tell her you're back and peddling whiskey to the Piutes.'

'Now why would you want to do that for?' Kerry asked. 'What's wrong with our original deal anyway?' He looked at Al Manners, still sitting there. 'Ain't you dead yet?'

'I'm hurt, Joe!'

'You don't look bad hurt to me,' Kerry said. He turned back to Graves. 'All right, so we had a little misunderstanding and George got burned a little, and Al got a bullet in him. Hell, we can't get along all the time. What's getting those two horse wranglers anyway? I want to do that as bad as you do, but I'd like to make a little money at the same time. It's a good bet they got a horse trap somewhere, and mustangs in it. They'd bring a good price at Fort Defiance.'

'A fifty-fifty split?' Graves asked.

Kerry shrugged. 'Why now, that's a little steep, but I guess I can go it. Graves, if you go it alone, it's two against one. Stick with me, and it's the other way around.'

'I don't trust you,' Harry Graves said.

Kerry laughed. 'Hell, I don't trust anybody. Tell you what, you pull out, do as we planned. I'll see if I can get the bullet out of Al and we'll join you in about five days.'

Graves thought about it, and for his answer

he backed away from the camp, got on his horse, and got out fast. George Manners was putting grease on his face; it was cherry red and would blister badly. Joe Kerry knelt by Al and unbuttoned his shirt to look at the wound. The small, underpowered bullet had caught him on the breastbone, and gone no farther; Kerry thought he could dig it out without carving Al up too badly.

'I want to kill him,' George Manners said sourly.

'He's mine,' Al said, sweating in spite of the chill in the air.

'Tell you what we'll do,' Kerry said softly. 'When the time comes, I'll count three and we'll all shoot him at the same time. Kick up that fire a little, George. I've got to cut this pill out before he gets lead poison.'

*   *   *

When Charlie Gannon rode into Jenny Regan's yard, he made a quick survey of the burned barn, then went on to the house and flung open the front door. He paused just inside, saw the smashed furniture, and the dried blood on the floor. 'Oh, no,' he said; it was a moan of ache and despair for he thought a natural thing, that the Indians had turned on her and killed her as they had killed her husband.

Angrily he kicked at the smashed furniture,

sending a broken chair crashing against the wall.

'Charlie?'

Her voice came from the bedroom and he plunged after it to stop in the doorway. She lay on the bed, her face melon-round, and when she saw him there she began to cry, silently, the tears large, a quick spilling down her cheeks. He came to her side with a rush and put his arms around her and she moaned, half from pain, half from the joy of having him with her.

'Shanti took Beans,' she said. 'They were all drunk, Charlie.'

'We'll get him back,' Gannon said fervently. Gently he lowered her back on the bed and went into the kitchen. He made a fire with the wood at hand, the smashed furniture, then went outside for a pail of water. While this heated, he rummaged around and found Adam Regan's shaving gear; she had it neatly put away with the rest of his things.

With a small pan of water and soap, he went into the bedroom. There was no need to explain to her what he was going to do; she knew that the wound had to be closed. He helped her sit up, propped her there with pillows and rolled blankets, then brought in the razor and stropped it on his belt. While he shaved around the wound, she uttered no outcry, but her hands dug into the bedcovers, and perspiration ran down her face.

Afterward he laid her back against the

headboard so she could rest; the tough part was yet ahead, sewing up the wound. Gannon didn't know much about these things although he'd performed some rough surgery in his time, for men had a habit of getting hurt a long way from the nearest doctor. He had hoped that Adam Regan had been a musical man and that there would be an old fiddle lying about; the E string, soaked in hot water, would do nicely, but Regan hadn't been talented that way.

Gannon finally settled on some silk thread he got by patiently picking apart a tie found among Regan's things; and as he threaded it through a needle, he couldn't help but think that Regan was still providing for her, in a rather round-about way.

It was too bad he had nothing to give her to ease the pain, and he hated to hurt her; each gasp was a thrust into his own body, but he closed the wound, bound her head with an old sheet ripped into four-inch strips, then settled her flat in bed and thought about straightening up the place, fixing her something to eat.

He killed a chicken late that afternoon, plucked it, and made a good broth for her. It was dark when he took it in to her, and he propped her up again and spooned it for her.

She felt like talking, and he let her; talk was good for a person.

'I needed you, Charlie. So I burned the barn down, hoping you'd see it.'

'Ben will be here tomorrow,' he said. 'I'll go get Beans then.' He took her hand and held it. 'He'll be all right. Shanti likes the boy, so he'll be all right.' He saw that she wanted to believe this, and tried to make it a little stronger, a little easier for her to believe. 'He's sober now, Jenny, and sorry for what he's done. Like as not he'll bring Beans back himself.'

'No,' she said. 'He'll be afraid of punishment. He'll believe the army will come after him and kill him.'

'But he'll trust you, Jenny. Here, eat some more broth.'

She swallowed, then said, 'Charlie, he'll be afraid. Go find him, Charlie. Please, I'll be all right.'

He shook his head. 'When Ben gets here to look after you, I'll go. Come on, finish your broth.'

'I don't want any more,' she said. 'Please, Charlie, go now. Shanti knows he did a bad thing, and if he were in my place he would not forgive me. So how can he really believe I would?' She didn't want to start crying again, and fought for a minute to keep the tears back. 'Shanti's spent all day sobering up, being sick, but right now he's cold sober and he's trying to think. By tomorrow noon, his camp will be deserted. That's why there's no time, Charlie. God knows where he'll go.'

'I'll find him,' Gannon assured her. 'Jenny, get some sleep now, if you can. I'll be in the other room.'

He covered her well and left the connecting door open, then stood in the big room wondering what mess he should clean up first. There wasn't a doubt in his mind that she was right about the Piute chief. Still, he had to think of her before the boy. He couldn't help himself there, for she was a woman and he was pretty sure that he loved her.

The boy would be all right; Shanti would be too scared now to do anything but take him along, and Gannon believed that he could find any new camp. He'd just keep hunting until he did find it.

As quietly as possible, he cleaned up the room, stacked the broken things outside, then went out to take care of his horse. He unsaddled and turned him into the corral, then carried his rifle and saddlebags into the house. He spread his blankets near the stove; he'd have to get up during the night to put wood in it to keep the house warm. And several times he looked in on Jenny, but she was quiet, lost in a restless, troubled sleep. It was too bad a man couldn't carry with him some of those pills the doctor had given him that time he broke his leg in two places. By the time they'd gotten him out of the hills and into the ranch house, he'd almost been out of his mind with pain, but two pills had put him to sleep around the clock.

Toward morning, the cold woke him and he

rebuilt the fire, then went into the bedroom to see how she was getting along. Her troubled dreams had made her thrash about; he pulled the blankets back over her and felt her face; she had a fever, all right, and it was going to get a lot worse.

Well, he'd kind of expected it; it always seemed that a fever came after a serious injury. He closed all the doors, except the one to her bedroom, and kept the fire built up to keep her warm, but by early morning he saw that wasn't going to work. He'd just have to move her and the bed into the big room, and that wasn't going to be any snap. He first built a pallet on the floor, and put her on this, then took the heavy bed apart and set it up in the other room. He made the covers up neatly and carried her to it; she didn't know she was being moved.

While he was outside bringing in wood, he saw a horseman and thought that it was Ben Clayton, coming a little early. On the second trip, he saw that it wasn't Ben at all and went in to get his rifle.

He didn't just barge right out again, but stood by the window and watched the man approach. Then he saw who it was, and the feeling that he'd been entertaining, that he'd seen this man before, made a lot of sense.

Harry Graves came into the yard and stepped down from his horse.

Charlie Gannon opened the door then and stepped out, and watched the surprise wash over Graves' face.

'Now ain't it a small world?' Gannon asked.

'What are you doing here?' Graves asked.

'You got it backwards,' Gannon said softly. 'Looking for something, Harry?'

'The Mormon woman,' Graves said. 'My business is with her.'

'Finish what you've got with me first,' Gannon said. 'You know, I can't help but thinkin' how odd it is, you popping up here, just at this time. Would you like to explain that, Harry?'

'No, I wouldn't care to,' Graves said, turning to his horse. 'My business with the woman can wait. See you, Charlie.'

'Now hold on a minute,' Gannon said flatly. 'The last time I saw you, you threatened me. I took it for talk, but here you are, out in the middle of nowhere, with no excuse for being here, except to come after me. I want to settle it now, Harry. I don't want to spend the rest of my life looking over my shoulder, just to see if you're there.'

'And suppose I don't want to settle it?'

Gannon frowned. 'Harry, I don't see that you've got a choice. I've got troubles of my own. I don't need you to make 'em worse.' He reached out and set the rifle against the door. 'I'll wait for you.'

'I like a better hand than this one,' Graves said.

'You play what's been dealt you,' Gannon

139

told him. 'Come on, Harry, I ain't got much time.'

He thought for a moment that Graves was going to back away from this, and was really wishing he would, but not holding out much hope for it. Graves snatched his rifle from the saddle boot, levered it and was swinging it up before Gannon unlimbered enough to reach for his own Winchester. Graves' shot splintered wood near Gannon's head; Gannon flopped, belly flat on the ground, pointed, and squeezed off.

Graves threw up both hands and tossed the rifle away from him as though he were sick and tired of it, then he just turned to wax in the saddle and fell to the ground. Gannon got up and walked over to him; Graves was still alive, but wouldn't be for long.

'For a man—who don't gamble, you—sure got good—hands,' he said.

'Beginner's luck,' Gannon said.

'Bury me deep,' Graves said, and died before Charlie Gannon could promise.

CHAPTER NINE

In mid-afternoon, a powder-fine snow began to fall, and Gannon rounded out the mound of earth that was Harry Graves' final resting place. Then he stood there, leaning on the shovel while the fresh dirt slowly turned white. He wondered whether he should say a few words over the man, but then decided not to, since he'd shot him.

It was a bad thing, Gannon thought, to shoot a man because you were in a hurry and didn't want to be bothered. And that's what it had amounted to, he knew. With Jenny to look after, and Beans to find, he just hadn't wanted to be bothered by Harry Graves.

So you just take your rifle and shoot a man.

Ben Clayton was coming across the flats and he pulled into the yard, swinging toward the barnyard when he saw Gannon. Clayton got down and stamped his feet, then looked at the fresh grave, and a touch of horrified shock blanched his complexion.

'My God, she isn't dead?'

'She's bad hurt and down with fever,' Gannon said. 'This is Harry Graves, Ben. I killed him.' He threw the shovel aside and turned toward the house. Quickly he sketched for Ben Clayton what had happened, and let the young man draw his own conclusions.

'Somehow I can't help but tie Harry Graves in with those drunk Indians,' Ben said. 'And when I think of whiskey, it brings to my mind Joe Kerry and those two brothers.'

'Well I sure ain't going to worry about 'em now,' Gannon said. 'Ben, I want you to stay here with Jenny. Watch her constantly, keep her warm, and try to get that fever to break. I guess you know what to do. You nursed me through a siege once.'

'Yeah,' Clayton said. 'You going after the boy?' He expressed his opinion with a shrug. 'The snow's started. Winter'll be set in good in another two weeks. And the Indians have one hell of a start on you. So what chance have you really got? You don't know this country that good.'

'You want me to forget it? Not make any try at all? Ben, if you were in my place, would you count the odds?'

'No, I wouldn't,' Ben Clayton said. 'Charlie, you won't get mad if I just talk right out to you?'

'Go ahead.'

'You stay here and let me find the boy.' He saw the resistance rise in Gannon's eyes, and went on quickly. 'Charlie, the cold gets in your bones too easily, and the steam is gone. There's a lot of miles out there, Charlie, a lot of hills to climb; Shanti ain't going to be sitting still. Let me go. I'm stronger than you.'

Gannon puffed his cheeks and made a wry face. 'There's no sense in letting my pride get out of hand now, Ben. Yeah, you can outrun me, outride me, outlast me all right. But I've got something inside me, Ben, that you don't have: I got a love for this woman and for the boy, because she loves him. That'll keep me going, Ben, no matter how far it is.' He took Clayton by the arm and led him inside.

142

Immediately he began to gather his gear together; he talked while he worked. 'I'll cut north of here. Jenny talked about neighbors. If I can, I'll send help back; you're going to need it.'

'What about our horses, Charlie?'

'Turn 'em loose for all I care,' Gannon said. He straightened up and looked at Ben Clayton. 'Is that going to be so hard to do, Ben? God, man, there'll be other times, other horses.' He went back to rolling his blankets. 'Give 'em to Joe Kerry if you want. I don't care.'

'I like to hang on to what's mine,' Clayton said. 'And don't blame me for feeling that way, Charlie.'

'Hell, I haven't the time. Someday I might argue with you over it, but not now.'

He turned and walked out to where his horse was tied, and Ben Clayton followed him. 'When will you be back, Charlie?'

'When I get back,' Gannon said, saddling up. He lashed his bulky gear in place and swung up.

'What'll I tell her when she comes around?'

'Tell her I'll be back,' Gannon said.

He started to lift the reins but Clayton put out his hand and stopped him. 'Charlie, if it turns out bad, and she don't—'

'Ben, it'd better not turn out bad,' Gannon said flatly. Then he smiled and slapped Clayton on top of the head, crushing the crown

143

of his hat. 'Ben, you're fussin' and frettin' like a kid. Try and cover up your age a little, will you?'

Then he spurred his horse out of the yard before Clayton could bring forth a hot reply, a denial even when he knew Gannon spoke the truth. How long does it take for a fella to grow up, Clayton wondered, and turned into the house; he knew the fire needed tending.

It snowed the rest of the day and on into the night, and since Ben got only snatches of rest, he kept a watch on the snowfall, noticing that the flakes grew bigger toward morning, and after a bland dawn, it was coming down in earnest. He wondered where Gannon was now, and it really didn't matter; he'd be cold and wet from the snow and miserable, and Ben Clayton couldn't help but feel a little glad that Gannon was out there instead of himself.

Fighting fever was unpleasant business, but Clayton kept himself in constant attendance, always making sure she was bundled up in every quilt in the house, and that the fire was hot enough to scald turkeys. He'd just have to wait it out; there wasn't any other choice. And somewhere in the scales, little weights were being added to decide whether she'd make it or not.

*   *   *

Aldrich Benson lived thirty-one miles north of

144

Jenny Regan's place, and Gannon found it at dawn; he had been moving blindly, letting the horse take him, for even a snow couldn't blanket a horse's nose when it detected hay and a sheltering barn.

Benson was a big, bearded man with four grown women around the house, and more kids than Gannon cared to count. There were no locks on his doors. He brought Gannon inside, seated him by the fire, and while two of the women took his coat and scarf and hat, another poured a steaming cup of coffee.

'Bad weather for a man to be out,' Benson said. He looked at Gannon's hat, a slight frown of confusion wrinkling his forehead. 'My home is your haven, brother.'

Gannon caught on then and said, 'Amen, brother.'

The women were his wives, he guessed, and the children his, and he didn't bother to sort them out. Benson had the questions in his mind, but the manners not to ask them right out. He left it up to Charlie Gannon, who took a moment longer just to thaw out.

'I came from the Widow Regan's place,' Gannon said. 'Sore trouble there, brother. The Indians carried off the boy and busted open the widow's head. She's in the care of a friend, but she's got the fever.' He looked at the women and some of the children who were nearly grown. 'She needs woman's care, brother.'

145

'The widow's a proud woman,' Benson said severely. 'When her husband was killed, I offered to take her into my home as my wife. Her marriage was childless, as you probably know, but through no fault of her own, I'm sure. A fine figure of a woman like that should be fertile.' The frown reappeared. 'But she rejected my kindness in a way that offended me sorely. I don't understand the woman, brother. She's a shade too independent, to my likes.'

'A good man who feeds her well, works her hard and gives her a child every year ought to take that out of her,' Gannon said, wondering which was more important, to get up and hit this man, or play him along for Jenny Regan's sake.

'Exactly,' Benson said, and smiled.

'Well, brother, she won't marry anyone if she dies. But if you helped her now, and she got well, no doubt she'd be properly grateful.'

'Wise words, brother,' Benson said, and immediately set about stirring up an activity such as Gannon had never seen before. Some of the children went out to harness up a team to the wagon while others gathered up the things they would need, and two of Benson's wives made ready to leave.

Benson never stirred from his place by the fire, and Gannon had to admire the man's ability to organize; from the looks of things, Gannon suspected that the women and kids did all the work while Aldrich Benson sat in the shade and congratulated himself on his good luck.

The wagon left, with the two women and four older girls; everyone waved and called to them, except Benson and Gannon, who still hugged the fire. And when Benson thought they'd had enough merry-making, he said, 'Close the door; you're making a sharp draught.' Benson rubbed his hands together. 'I have some peach brandy, if you'd like a glass, brother.'

Gannon wanted to be going, but he thought it best not to refuse. The drinks were brought to the fire by one of the women, and Benson sipped his. 'You haven't told me where you're from and where you're bound, brother.'

So he finally asked it, Gannon thought. 'I'm just from the widow's place, and I'm bound to hunt for the boy until I find him.' He tossed off his drink and stepped to the door. 'Thank you, brother.'

'I'll go out with you,' Benson said. 'Fetch my coat, Bertha.'

He joined Gannon as he was about to mount. Benson saw the rifle in the saddle boot and that frown came back. 'Do you bear arms, brother? What kind of a believer are you?'

'I didn't say I was a Mormon,' Gannon told him. 'That was your conclusion.'

'Well, the hat—'

'A gift from Jenny Regan,' Gannon said,

147

lifting the reins. 'Don't be so quick to judge, Mr. Benson, and be more tolerant when you do.' Then he laughed. 'I never did believe the devil had horns. Did you?'

'Have you taken up with the Regan woman?' Benson asked. 'If you have, it's a sin a decent man could not forgive.' Then he stepped back a pace. 'But it's not for me to judge, is it, brother?'

'No, brother, it ain't.'

As he rode away, putting Benson's place behind him, Gannon felt a flood of relief; Jenny would have help now, woman help, which would mean more than a man's love, or even a doctor's advice.

He had wasted time, finding the Benson place, but he considered it worthwhile if for nothing else than his own peace of mind. With just Ben there, he'd have fretted and divided his attention, half on her and half on what he had to do, and none of it would have been any good. This way, with women there, she'd be all right. It took a woman to take care of the sick; he believed they were better than doctors, who were fine for giving anthrax shots, bringing in babies, and setting bones. Nursing required a special touch, a tenderness that only a woman possessed.

Gannon wasn't an Indian fighter, like some men who made a career of it, yet he had picked up a sound knowledge of Indians from just being around them and horse hunting in

Indian country. Shanti's camp had been a day north of Jenny's place; he knew that much. That was a day in good weather; he figured the snow and reduced visibility would double that time. Tomorrow then, he ought to be somewhere near the old camp; he'd start looking for high ground with water, and perhaps pick up the trail from there. It didn't seem likely though, with the snow blotting out everything.

But it was a starting place, and a man had to have that no matter what he tackled. Even Shanti had to have that, and Gannon supposed it would be the sure knowledge that he'd done something real bad that would cause him to make tracks before someone came after him with a rope. Well, where would a man go if he wanted to hide? Gannon wasn't sure, but he figured it would be rough country, and the farther away the better. Like as not, Gannon thought, he'll join up with some other tribe to hide the real reason for his 'visit.' The Utes liked the desert country but that was too open for Shanti. Well, he could rip out a big circle to the south into the Apache stronghold.

That sounded more likely. So Gannon made his camp and hoped the snow would stop and the clouds would lift so he could unlimber his telescope and have a look at the worst of the badlands. That would be his destination.

*　　　*　　　*

149

Captain Anders led his thirty-man patrol across the last stretch of white desert toward Jenny Regan's place. He had been there twice before, in years past, and rather liked to use her spring as a camp.

As he approached, he saw activity around her place and he rode forward with his sergeant only a few paces behind him. Ben Clayton came to meet him and as Anders dismounted, Clayton said, 'I'm real surprised to see you, Captain. What are you doing here?'

'Looking for you and Gannon,' Anders said. He took off his gloves and blew into his cupped hands. 'Is Mrs. Regan around?'

'Well, she is, but she's not feeling up to company.' Then Clayton told Anders of the kidnaping and Jenny Regan's injury. He jerked his thumb toward the house. 'Some Mormon folks from up the valley came night before last. I was about at the end of my string, I can tell you.'

'Yes, I can imagine.' Anders turned to the sergeant. 'Make a camp over by the spring, Sergeant. I'm sure it's all right.' Then he took Ben by the arm. 'Where's Gannon?'

'Out huntin' the Indians,' Clayton said. 'He's trying to find the boy.'

'In this weather? A tough job.'

'He knows it,' Ben said. 'Say, how come you're looking for us?'

'The commanding officer got a letter about ten days ago, or closer to two weeks—I always lose track of time in this country. Some woman

150

from Lordsburg wrote it, a Miss Mildred Jennings. Do you know her?'

'Well, yeah, I do,' Clayton admitted. 'But she's more Gannon's friend than mine. How come she wrote?'

'She was pretty much concerned about the threats Harry Graves made the night he had his trouble, and she thought the army ought to know that Graves had sworn to kill you, so if you turned up missing, we'd have an idea where to send the marshal. Have you seen Graves? He stopped at the post, and I gathered from his talk that there was bad blood.'

'Harry's dead,' Clayton said. 'He and Charlie shot it out some days ago.' He nodded toward the area where the barn used to stand. 'He's buried over there.'

'I see,' Anders said gravely. 'I suppose it was a fair fight?'

Clayton shrugged. 'Charlie said it was. And I found a bullet mark in the doorframe, so I guess Harry shot first.' He reached out and tapped Anders on the chest. 'But you didn't make the trip for nothin', Captain. Charlie and I figure that Graves had something to do with the Indians gettin' drunk.'

'Any proof?'

'No more than that I know a skunk makes a peculiar stink.'

Anders laughed. 'Your point is well taken, Clayton. As a matter of fact, Graves was talking very friendly-like to Joe Kerry and the

151

Manners boys back at Defiance. And I've always claimed that Joe bought favors from the Indians with jugs of whiskey.' He thought about it a minute, then nodded. 'All right, Clayton, we'll take up the trail of Kerry and his friends and see what comes of it.' He blew out a frosty breath. 'This is damned miserable weather though. Did you trap any horses?'

'Some,' Ben Clayton said. 'Charlie wants me to turn 'em loose; I can't handle the herd by myself. Like as not they've got every bit of vegetation grazed out of that canyon by now, so I guess I don't have much choice.'

'That's too bad,' Anders said politely, but he didn't act as though he really cared. 'Since you've got a stake in this, so to speak, you ought to come along.'

Clayton thought about this, then said, 'If it wasn't for *her* everything would be all right. Charlie and I could have taken care of everything.'

'Why, man, you're not blaming Jenny Regan, are you?' He took Clayton by the arm again, much the same as a father would to command complete attention from a son. 'We all have our share of bad luck, Clayton, but we don't look around to see who we can blame for it. A man looks to himself for answers, not to someone else to blame.' He dropped his hand. 'In the morning, I'll split my command. Sergeant Brusso can take a ten-man detail and round up Joe Kerry while I take the rest of the men and try and pick up Gannon's trail. He's got no business being alone now.'

'I'll go with you,' Ben Clayton said quickly.

'You'll stay here,' Anders said firmly. And when Clayton opened his mouth to object, Anders held up his hand. 'I don't like to say this, Clayton, but this is a military exercise and a civilian has no place in it.'

'Well, now ain't that just peachy?' Clayton said. 'What's to keep me from tagging along a mile behind?'

'Your pride,' Anders told him bluntly. 'You've got the manner of a man who has to win before he'll play the game. I'm sorry, Clayton. We can't make those kind of guarantees. You stay here; the women need some protection.'

'Now I didn't like the way you said that!'

'So we have a thin skin too. You are somewhat of a problem to yourself, aren't you?'

He turned his head as though to yell at one of his men, and Clayton hit him. The blow was sudden, a product of anger, and Ben hadn't intended to catch Anders off guard; it might appear that he was looking for an advantage.

Anders' campaign hat flew off and he fell in the snow. Then he looked at Ben Clayton and said, 'You're excused, son.'

'I'm excused what?' He doubled his fists. 'Don't tell me to go to my room, damn it!'

Sergeant Brusso came over on the run,

helped Anders to his feet, then said, 'Shall I take care of this, sir?'

'Forget it,' Anders said. 'Well, Clayton, what are you standing there for?'

'I'm waiting for my fight,' Clayton said. 'Do I get one or not?'

'You do not,' Anders said calmly.

'What's the matter, you scared?'

Brusso would have hit him if Anders hadn't flung out his arm and blocked him off. Anders said, 'When a man thinks a fight is useless, Mr. Clayton, you can't insult him into changing his mind.' He bent and picked up his hat, slapped the snow off it, and put it on his head.

Then he turned and walked away to the soldier camp, leaving Clayton and Sergeant Brusso standing there. Ben swayed as though he thought seriously of taking out after him, but Brusso shook his head.

'The captain would eat you alive, if he thought it would do any good, mister. Better let this drop. He doesn't have to prove anything by fighting you.'

'Yeah, then maybe I'll prove something by fighting him,' Ben snapped.

Brusso smiled. 'Son, we can see that. Now behave yourself.'

Clayton remained in that spot while Brusso joined the captain, then Ben wheeled and stomped through the snow to the house. One of the Benson girls was gathering up wood, clacking the pieces together to shed the snow.

'Don't be angry,' she said softly. 'It doesn't do any good.'

He stopped and looked at her, closely this time, because he had an excuse to. She was rather short, a little too plump, but her face was a mirror of sweetness; he suspected that she had never entertained a bad thought about anyone.

'Louise, I thought you women never mixed in a man's business?'

'Sometimes it's hard to stay out,' she said. He started to take the load of wood from her arms and she battled him with a polite stubbornness.

'What's the matter with you?' he asked. 'I was only trying to help you.'

'It's a woman's work,' she said quickly, hoping he would let it go at that. But he wouldn't. Already he'd suffered one humiliating defeat and he'd be hanged if he'd take another from a woman. He grabbed the wood and roughly jerked it from her arms, almost spilling her to her knees.

Her mother came out then, just in time to see the tail end of the struggle, and she misread it completely. Quickly she walked up to the girl and slapped her face. 'Now you get in that house!' Her voice was like the cut of a whip. 'The idea! Fauchin' around with a man in broad daylight.' She gave Ben Clayton a scathing look. 'It's bad enough being in this house of—of fallen grace, without having a man maul young girls.' She shook her finger under Ben Clayton's nose. 'Now you keep your distance. One more thing, and we'll leave.'

'Is that a promise?' Ben asked. He turned then and went into the house. Louise was at the stove making some stew, and Ben Clayton walked over to her, took her by the arm and turned her so that she faced him.

'Have you ever been kissed properly?' He could see by the sudden flood of color in her face that she had never been, properly or not. 'It's time you found out then,' he said and quickly folded her in his arms. Their lips met for just a moment, but it was enough to melt the anger in him, enough to make him sorry he had hurt her just to get at her mother.

The Benson women were quite shocked, and Louise's mother moaned as though she had been fatally stabbed, then she gathered her righteousness like a cloak and said, 'All right, young man, you'll find that I meant what I said. Gather our things; we're leaving.'

Louise looked hurt and puzzled. 'She's still sick, Ma!'

'Where's this here Christian charity?' Ben asked.

The older woman turned her dark eyes on him and said, 'I have it, young man, but it is not your privilege to test it. We've been here too long as it is; my own work has suffered enough.'

'He did it out of hurt, Ma,' Louise said

quickly.

'Now don't make excuses for me!' Ben Clayton said. 'Dang it all, do you think I'd fall down if I didn't have something to lean on?'

'Go if you want, Ma,' Louise said. 'I can't. Not until Jenny Regan is well.'

'Now look,' Ben said. 'I didn't mean to start a family fuss. I'm sorry for what I did. I was mad, and I didn't think.' Begging was hard for him, because it meant putting a need before his pride. But he did it then, and didn't feel too bad about it. 'Mrs. Benson, I'm really sorry. Stay. I'll keep out of the house and away from Louise.'

Mrs. Benson looked at him a moment, then said in a softer voice, 'I didn't name it a sin to kiss Louise, young man. But it was wrong to do it for the reasons you had.' Then she turned to the others. 'I think Jenny's fever is down enough to allow a bath. Out, young man! Go on now. You'll be called for supper.'

'I'm truly sorry,' Ben said. 'Louise is a nice girl.'

'You don't have to tell me that,' Mrs. Benson said. 'Boy, how long has it been since somebody's taken a strap to you?'

'I—I beg your pardon?' he stammered.

'Some people just have to be strapped regularly,' she said, 'or they're not fit to have around. And you've got all the signs.'

She closed the door, and Ben Clayton stood there for a time, thinking about that. By golly,

157

Gannon must have known that, because there'd been times when he had really laid it on, and pretty regularly too.

It made Ben feel a little foolish to think about it, but to his surprise, he didn't feel the rise in temper which usually went along with things like that.

CHAPTER TEN

When the weather cleared, Gannon took up the hunt again, trying to stay in the high ground so he could use his telescope. He often sat for an hour at a time, examining the surrounding country with infinite care, then he would move to another position, and take another long look from this new angle.

Two days of searching netted him nothing except a sore back from sleeping on rocks. He wished he could remember what it was like to feel warm; the memory of it might drive some of the chill from him. It seemed that all the fractures and sprains he had collected in his life became focal points for their own bit of misery, and he wished Ben was with him, not to share the discomfort, but to remind him that a man had to keep going and not give in to these things.

It was a funny way to be missing a man, Gannon thought as he moved along. But then he guessed he just did better when Ben was around. That young fella would just jump out of his blankets on a frosty morning, dash about in his underwear and build a fire, and laugh all the time he was doing it, and it was kind of a tonic to Gannon, a tonic he missed, for with Ben around he'd always bit back the groan that rose when he stirred suddenly.

Yes, he just did better with Ben there, and he missed him now.

On a high piece of ground, Gannon dismounted to have a look through the glass, and while he scanned the bleak land he thought of the talk he and Ben had had back in Lordsburg, about how foolish it was to try to winter out in a strange country. Dog gone kid never listened to anything a man said and good advice was like water poured on sand; it just went on through and never left a trace behind. If they'd stayed in Lordsburg, he'd be sleeping at the stable, drinking his glass of whiskey now and then and living like a man ought to live, among people, not rocks and desert and more trouble than he could handle.

He thought of Jenny; he wouldn't have known her if he hadn't given in to Ben. But what did that matter? What a man didn't know didn't hurt him. No man knew what lay over the hill for him; he just climbed what was in front of him and hoped there was good waiting for him.

Gannon stared a long time at one particular

spot, then snapped the telescope shut and mounted his horse. Pulling down off the higher ground, he began to work his way to lower levels, through snow-clogged defiles, and finally into the valley floor. He followed it for an hour, then swung to the right, passed through a short canyon and eased his way up a long, winding slope.

The Indian camp was crowded in between rock prominents, completely hidden from anyone passing through the valleys. But only a man taking the high country, and with binoculars, could have found it as Gannon had.

He rode boldly into it and two dogs raced out and snapped at the horse's heels. Several of the men appeared and presented stony expressions as he dismounted and walked over to them. He examined their faces carefully, to see if he could recognize any that had come with Shanti to Jenny's place, but he could not. The visit had been brief and his attention had been on other matters, so the best he could hope for was that they recognized him.

One of the Indians stood alone, a robe over his shoulders, a blanket wrapped tightly around his waist. Gannon said, 'I come to talk with Shanti.'

'I am the brother of Shanti,' the Indian said. 'Speak with me.'

'Where's Shanti?'

'Gone. Big hunt.'

'In winter?' Gannon shook his head. 'He's

here, hiding from me.'

'Shanti hides from no man!'

'Then why is he gone? Why did the chief move his camp?'

'Spring dry up.'

Gannon paused a moment, then took out his tobacco and rolled a smoke with cold-stiffened fingers. He handed the tobacco to the Indian, who put some in his mouth to chew. After lighting his cigaret, Gannon said, 'Tell Shanti the Mormon woman lives. The blow on the head did not kill her. She wants the boy back. I've come for him.'

'No boy here,' the Indian said. 'Shanti on hunt.' He motioned to the north. 'Big hunt.'

It was, Gannon knew, a damned lie, but he wasn't quite sure what he should do about it. He puffed on his cigaret and thought about it. He could pretend to believe it, leave the camp, and end up about where he had started. Or he could hang around a few days and get on their nerves and hope for something to break. Indians were liars when it came to dealing with white men, but their lies were often so simple and childish that anyone could see through them.

'My horse is tired,' Gannon said at last. 'I'll stay and rest him up.'

'No food,' the Indian said. 'No stay.'

Gannon smiled. 'I'll eat my own food. I only want to share a lodge and a fire, friend.' He looked around the camp and saw their faces,

161

completely unreadable, but maybe a little worried. And he didn't see any of the women or kids; they were being kept out of sight for some reason. 'What you got to be afraid of?' he asked.

'No 'fraid,' the Indian said. 'But Shanti no come back 'til snow gone.'

'I can't wait that long,' Gannon said regretfully. 'You say he went north?'

'Go far. That way.' Again he pointed north. 'Long hunt.'

'Went alone, huh?' Gannon looked around at the braves. 'I never knew an Indian to hunt alone. You sure he didn't go south to meet up with Apaches?'

'No Apaches. Go that way.'

Gannon shrugged and went to his horse for his blanket roll and saddlebags; he took his rifle along too, for leaving it on the saddle might create more suspicion than if he took it with him.

He came back and said, 'If the Mormon woman gets the boy back, Shanti won't be punished. You ought to tell him that.'

'Not here. No boy here.'

'Then Shanti took him along,' Gannon said. 'Indian, if that boy's been hurt, I'm going to find Shanti, gut him out with my knife and wear his damned hide for a vest.'

'You alone,' the Indian said. 'We many. Maybe you die here.'

'Maybe,' Gannon said. 'Ain't you Shanti's

162

brother? I thought the Mormon woman saved your life once. Do you pay her back like this? Stealing her child?' He laughed. 'You kill me, Indian, and the army will hunt you like a mountain cat and you'll hang at the end of a rope.' He let the effect of this sink in a bit, then decided to go all the way, Indian style. He knew how strongly they believed in medicine, and he made a little of his own. 'You want me to tell you what I saw?' He reached into the saddlebag and got out his telescope. Then he extended it and handed it to the Indian, and he looked through it and brought a distant point of land. Before the Indian had a chance to get over the wonder of it, or figure it out, Gannon took it away from him and restored it to the saddlebag. 'With this I see everything, Indian. All white men have such a thing; they see all. With it I saw one white man, named Graves, come to your camp with whiskey. You drank the whiskey, and when your brain wheeled and you could barely stand, you got on your horses and rode to the Mormon woman's house. Shanti led you.'

A gasp of surprise escaped the men standing there and they looked at each other. Gannon kept his expression neutral although the payoff of this sudden idea staggered him, elated him.

'The woman fought. Her clothes were torn. The things in the house were smashed and the boy was taken. Then whiskey wore off and Shanti thought of the thing he had done. You

163

moved your camp the next day, but I found it. Through this glass I saw it all, saw this camp, and came here. The soldiers have such a glass and saw it all. They see me here now, talking to you, and if I am struck they will see that, too, and pick out the man who did it.' He reached out and touched the Indian on the chest. 'I saw Shanti leave here with the boy. He did not go north to hunt. He went south, to speak to his friends among the Apaches, to sell the boy so that he will be hidden and Shanti cannot be blamed.'

This last was a guess, but he saw from their faces that it had been an x-ring bulls-eye.

Shanti's brother said, 'It is as you say; he has gone to sell the boy.'

Gannon almost asked when, then caught himself; he was supposed to know when. He'd have to use another ruse here. 'It is as I saw,' he said. 'You will come with me to the Apache land. You will see that I am accepted as a friend and that no harm comes to me. If this isn't done, the army will come, for they will have seen it all.'

'Shanti will not be pleased.'

'No harm will come to any of you if the boy is brought back unharmed,' Gannon said. 'We will leave now.'

He wanted to say that they would leave in the morning, after he'd had some warm food and a warm sleep, but he had to press this now, had to push it along before anyone had a

164

chance to think it over. As it stood, the Indians thought he had a bit of magic and they were afraid of it, and if he could keep them thinking that, they wouldn't harm him or do anything against him.

'You will take ten men,' Gannon said. 'We'll go now. I'm ready. The boy must be brought back.' He brought out the telescope and started to extend it, and the Indians gasped; they didn't like to see someone fool around with big medicine in their presence.

The camp became very active then; horses were caught up and ten braves readied themselves for a long ride. Gannon stood there, the telescope in his hands. He'd probably have to carry it in the open now, to remind them to behave, and he wondered if that St. Louis mail-order house ever thought of this application for their six-dollar looking glass.

*   *   *

Captain Anders split his command, moved northward with his segment, and left the remainder in command of Sergeant Brusso who wasted no time leaving the Regan place.

Ben Clayton knew that the Mormon women were relieved to see them go; they did not trust men out of their faith, it seemed, and Ben couldn't blame them for it. He wasn't much on religion himself, but it had a lot of good points,

165

especially calling on the decency in people rather than letting their native meanness go unchecked. He knew he could sure stand some of it; maybe it would curb his temper and his intolerance.

He sure had made a fool of himself with the Benson woman, kissing Louise like that, just to make her mother mad. There ought to be a time soon when he'd outgrow those foolish impulses; Gannon didn't get into those predicaments all the time.

With the soldiers gone, Ben Clayton felt sharply this 'manless' place; he was not at all at ease around women, for he couldn't shake the notion that they talked about him when he wasn't listening and watched too closely for the mistakes he was about to make. He kept thinking about Gannon, out there somewhere, and he kept wishing to hell that he was there too; anything would be better than this. Dog gone it, since those Mormon women showed up, he really didn't know how Jenny was getting along; they acted like it was none of his business.

Well, maybe it wasn't really, but she was his concern because Gannon had made her so, and he ought to know about these things.

So he went to the house and knocked on the door. Mrs. Benson answered it, appearing neither friendly nor unfriendly; Ben didn't know how to take her at all.

'How's Jenny?' Ben asked. Then he

166

remembered to take off his hat.

This seemed to mark some increase in approval, some progress in the training of Benjamin Clayton, for a bit of warmth came into her eyes.

'She is improving steadily,' she said, 'with only a little fever coming back at night. I think she'll be up in a few days. But no hard work for her, do you understand?'

'Yes'm, I understand.'

The Benson woman was all business. 'Did you round up the stock she kept in the barn?'

'They're in the corral.'

'Wood's cut?' He nodded. 'Then you can come in for a minute. Wipe your feet first; I have enough to do without scrubbing floors on account of an untidy man.' She opened the door and closed it after him. 'She's in the bedroom.'

He went in and found her in bed, covers to her chin. Jenny Regan smiled at him, and he was surprised to see her so thin, her face so drawn. The swelling in her cheek and eye had gone down, but there was a large discoloration. The bandage made a white cap on her head.

'They told me you were here, Ben,' she said. 'Any word from Charlie?'

'No, nothing.'

'How many days has it been?'

He shrugged. 'I've lost count, Jenny. Charlie will bring the boy back.'

'You sound so sure; I almost believe you.'

167

'He's not the kind who quits, or fails to do what he sets out to do.'

She seemed very sad, full of regrets. 'I've ruined things for you, Ben, and I'm terribly sorry. Nothing has worked out the way you wanted it to.'

'I guess it can't always be the way a man wants it,' Ben said. Then he shrugged. 'Anyway, it looks like we'd be sittin' in camp with our herd, if nothin' else. I didn't think the winters were so danged cold here.'

'Spring always comes,' Jenny said. 'What then?'

He shrugged again, then said, 'I'm gettin' like Charlie; I don't want to think that far ahead.' Then he laughed. 'Darned if it didn't get turned around somehow. Charlie, now, he's always been the one who didn't give a hang about tomorrow, and I've always lived a day ahead of myself. But right now I'll bet he's thinkin' about buildin' a new barn in the spring and gettin' a crop in, and maybe enlargin' the place, since a man'll be workin' it. But I don't want to even think about spring.'

'Spring means good-bye,' she said softly. 'You know that, Ben. He'll stay and you won't. Will good-bye be so hard to say?'

'I don't know,' he admitted. 'I never thought about sayin' it.'

Mrs. Benson knocked lightly. 'Let her rest now.'

He went into the other room; there was a

168

place being set at the table and Louise was bringing a platter of food from the stove. Mrs. Benson said, 'You must be tired of your own cooking, Ben. I never knew a man yet who really liked backfat and cold beans. Sit down.'

This sudden kindness surprised him, but he didn't turn it down. He placed boiled potatoes on his plate, smothered them in gravy and sided them with some beef. Louise placed a bowl of stewed tomatoes by his plate, and smiled briefly when he thanked her with a glance.

'I've got nothing against talk,' Mrs. Benson said. 'Pull up a chair if you've a mind to, Louise.'

Ben Clayton turned and looked at the woman. 'I don't know if you're for me or against me.'

'We're not against anyone,' Mrs. Benson said, then herded the others into the chores; she believed that everything had to be scrubbed and properly set in place, and couldn't rest until it was.

'It must be cold in the tool shed,' Louise said softly.

'Well I don't mind the cold so much, but it's no fun talkin' to a shovel,' Ben said. 'I keep worryin' about them answerin' me back.' He laughed softly because he felt good and was a little ashamed of some of the things he'd thought about these women.

'Why do you wear that gun?' Louise asked.

'Are you afraid?'

'No, I ain't afraid. Well, it's just that a man never knows what he'll run into.'

'Thou shalt not kill,' Louise told him.

'Now just because I carry a gun don't mean I go around killing people with it,' Ben said. Then he frowned and sorted out his thoughts before speaking again. 'I don't know why it is, but I keep getting the feeling that no matter what I do, you're going to see wrong in it and keep pointing it out to me.' He pushed back his half-eaten meal. 'I think I'd better go back to the shed.'

He didn't slam the door when he went out, although he had an impulse to, and he spent the rest of the day purging himself of this new irritation by hard work. By dark he had most of the burned rubble cleaned off the stone foundation. The metal was sorted out of the ashes and could be used again in the spring when Gannon started to build.

Ben just couldn't see himself as a farmer, but he knew this would make a nice horse ranch, if a man fenced off the blind canyon back of the place. While he cooked his supper over the small sheet-iron fireplace he'd made, he thought about all the things he and Charlie Gannon could do with this place. Why, they could spend the summer and spring trapping horses, gentle them for a drive in the fall, and maybe make two thousand dollars apiece. Jenny and the boy could go right on working their small farm, raising the table fare and some hay; it sure would work out fine, and it wouldn't take much talking to get Charlie to see it either.

As he settled for the night, he felt better; the old optimism was coming back, and things really hadn't changed so much. Charlie wouldn't kick him out, not after five years.

They'd go right on being partners, whether Jenny liked it or not.

He finished the clean-up job by late afternoon the next day, then, as he was putting the tools away, he saw Sergeant Brusso and his detail coming across the desert floor; he had their horses tied together, and a tough job driving them.

Ben opened the corral gate when they came into the yard and Brusso's men herded them in.

The sergeant came over and said, 'From the looks of things, some cat got three. We had to shoot two more. You'd better keep a watch at night. Must be poor pickings with so much snow in the hills. The cat's liable to show up again.'

'I sleep in the shed,' Clayton said. 'So I'll hear anything—'

'That ain't good enough when a cat's got his wind up for horses,' Brusso said. 'I'll leave some lanterns with you. Hang 'em on the four corner poles, and a few in between if you got enough lanterns. Burn 'em all night. Cats don't like light. It may save you a few horses.'

'I'll do that, and I sure thank you for bringing 'em here. I'd hate to lose 'em now.'

'Two of my troopers will be along later with your buckboard and gear,' Brusso said. He blew out a frosty breath and rubbed his unshaven face. 'I hope this weather holds for a few more days. Kind of like to get started finding Joe Kerry's camp. Like as not he's holed up near here.' He turned his head first one way, then the other, surveying the bleak land and the rocky buttes sitting like brown biscuits in a pan of flour. 'Another foot of snow and I won't worry about Kerry going anyplace. Like as not the badlands east of here are clogged.'

'He does business with the army,' Clayton said. 'He wouldn't fight you.'

'No, he wouldn't,' Brusso admitted. 'But we never liked doing business with him, Clayton. But who the hell else was there? Joe Kerry scared off every horse-hunting outfit there was, until you and Gannon came along.' He looked again at the barren country. 'No, Joe will be holed up somewhere, snug as a tick in a quilt. Some high ground someplace out there, where he can see what goes on below. I know the man. He's got good Indian sense, which works against us now.'

'Harry Graves must have known where his camp was,' Clayton said. 'Charlie turned his horse into the corral and put his gear in the shed. I never looked at it, and I guess he didn't either. You think we should?'

'I'd like to see it,' Brusso said and followed Clayton to the shed.

Graves' saddle and bedroll were in the corner. Brusso spread the bedroll on the floor.

'Two blankets,' he said. 'No ground cloth though. What could that mean?' He thought a moment, his heavy lips pursed. 'Could be that when he left Kerry's camp for here, it was just one day's ride. Graves figured to stay here the night and go back the next day.'

The sergeant opened the sack carrying Graves' food and cooking pots. 'A skillet, half pound of bacon, and some coffee.' He looked at Ben Clayton. 'Not much for a man on the trail, is it?'

'Hell, I carry more than that all year around,' Clayton said. 'But Graves was a city man, Sergeant. He wouldn't know what to have along.'

Brusso shook his head. 'He had enough sense to find Shanti's camp with the whiskey, so I've got to give him credit for knowing his way around. Besides, he was with Kerry for some weeks before they got here. Graves wasn't stupid, from what I hear.'

'So you think Kerry's not far away?'

Brusso nodded and left the shed. On the way back to his horse, he said, 'I'd like to leave a couple of men here with you, Clayton, but I just can't spare 'em.'

'I'll make out.'

'How are you fixed for arms and ammunition?'

'I got a rifle and a box of shells, and this pistol.' He ran his fingers around the shell belt to count the cartridges remaining. 'Sixteen there. Do I need any more?'

'I don't know what you're going to need,' Brusso said. 'Has the Mormon woman got a gun in the house?'

'She's got a shotgun,' Clayton said, smiling. 'I know that for danged sure because she pointed at me real business-like once.'

'You keep that in the house,' Brusso said. He took out his own .45 caliber Colt and handed it to Ben Clayton. 'You take this; I'll give you forty rounds to go with it. I'll take your pistol and what ammunition you have. Now I'd keep the Colt on; it ought to fit the holster if you cut out the bottom so that the barrel will stick through.'

'What is all this?' Clayton asked, pleasantly puzzled.

Brusso declined to answer. 'I'll leave a carbine and some shells also. I'd put them somewhere near the corral so I could get at them if I was cut off from my own rifle; I assume you'll leave that in the house.'

'No, I keep it with me, but I'll put it there if it'll make you any happier,' Clayton said.

Brusso wasn't amused at all. 'You'd better take this seriously.'

'Oh, I am! What's it supposed to be?'

'Joe Kerry and those tough brothers he always has tagging along,' Sergeant Brusso said carefully. 'Yeah, I know, you licked them once, but that was with fists, Clayton. You're all alone here, so you'd better be well armed no matter where you are, inside or out.'

Some of the amusement faded from Ben Clayton's mind, and he looked carefully at the sergeant. 'If you think Kerry's going to come here, why don't you hang around and help me?'

'If I hang around, he won't come,' Brusso said. 'He'll see us leave, or find it out soon enough. With luck, we might be able to come around behind him in time to give you some support. But don't count on it. Figure to play this alone, so play it smart.'

'Yeah,' Clayton said, beginning to get the whole picture. 'You've been playing it smart too, ain't you? Bringing my horses here just wasn't the result of a soft heart. You're setting me up as bait, so Kerry can take a crack at me *and* the horses.'

Brusso shrugged. 'Well, what's the matter with that? You ask yourself, Clayton, just what good are you except as bait?'

CHAPTER ELEVEN

It was nearly noon the next day by the time Ben Clayton got around to carrying the

175

firewood to the house, and then he saw his rifle sitting outside. He knocked with the toe of his boot, went on in when one of the Benson women opened the door, and dumped the armload into the wood box.

'What's my rifle doing outside?' he asked.

He spoke to Louise, but she shook her head, then her mother came out of Jenny Regan's room and shut the door.

'I put it there,' she said. 'We don't like firearms in the house, or anywhere.'

'It was put there for a reason,' Ben said patiently. 'Now I'd appreciate it if you left it alone.' He stepped outside, brought it in and placed it by the stove. Mrs. Benson's frown was an irritation to him. 'Lady, I don't tell you how to run the house, do I? Then don't tell me how to run our affairs.'

He went out before she could say anything, feeling that certainly she had something to say; they were well versed in argument, and pretty good ones at that.

Work kept him busy that day. Late in the afternoon he could feel the threat of more snow in the air. Just before dark he took a cruise toward the house to see if his rifle was sitting outside or not. It wasn't, and he felt pretty good about it; maybe he'd sounded more firm than he'd thought. Well, he decided, it was about time he began to sound assertive. One of the major troubles in his life stemmed from that damned freckled face and a voice

176

that just wasn't going to deepen; people couldn't seem to take him seriously, and that led to fights and some violent disagreements.

He guessed he'd got it across to the Benson-woman-boss; Ben Clayton was running things whether she liked it or not.

By the time he got the horses taken care of and his lanterns filled and brightly hung on their poles, it was late, and he went to the shed to eat and bed down.

It was good to be able to lie there and hear the horses moving about. Good because it meant that a man was at least getting something for all this trouble. They might end up with twenty-five head, and at thirty dollars apiece, that wasn't bad. Not as good as Ben Clayton wanted it, but he was learning to settle for less than he wanted.

He never did sleep soundly, and when he woke up suddenly he knew there was a reason. Quickly he shed his blankets, slipped into his coat and cracked the shed door for a look around. The wind was a sigh across the desert, husking powdered snow along before it, but there were no other sounds.

His first thought was that the damned cat had come back; once they found a good meal they made hogs of themselves. Ben eased out of the shed, his pistol in his hand, wishing he'd left that in the house and had the rifle instead.

Hunkered down, he could see the corral and the lanterns veiled by swirling snow. He didn't see anything wrong, yet he knew something was not right, and he hunched down there, thinking about it.

In some way, this was out of focus to him, like the fuzzy image he got through Gannon's telescope when he didn't extend the sections all the way. Then Clayton saw one of the far lanterns go out and he knew what was wrong; that was the second lantern out, and it was no accident.

Leaving the shed, he ran bunched up, staying a little way from the corral, and bellied down in the snow to wait. He wasn't looking at the lantern that had just gone out, but the next one down the line, the one he expected to go out next.

His wait wasn't long. Through the gauze of drifting snow he saw the man reach for the near lantern. Clayton sighted the best he could along the barrel of the pistol and triggered it off. The bullet pulverized the lantern, missing the man completely, and Ben swore heartily.

There was no doubt in his mind now who was out there; Kerry and his friends had come to steal the horses. From the far end of the corral, a stab of gunfire brightened the night, and the bullet passed somewhere in front of Clayton. He rolled and then streaked for the corral gate where he had the army carbine hidden; a man needed a lot more than a short gun for this work.

The man on the other side opened up good, levering his rifle as fast as he could, and what the fire lacked in accuracy, it made up in volume. Ben Clayton couldn't weather it; he simply had to move back and forget the rifle.

All this shooting brought lights on inside the house, and he hoped that they wouldn't come out to see what it was all about. The house was his last outpost of defense for it was strongly built, and inside it he could hold off six men. But not if those foolish women ran out to see what was going on and let Kerry or one of the others inside.

He forgot about getting the rifle and settled for what he had. The lanterns were working against him now; he couldn't get closer to the corral without being seen, and Kerry was already entrenched somewhere around the yard.

Best to sit quietly and think this one over, Ben decided. No use shooting up all his cartridges when he couldn't see anything to shoot at.

Then it occurred to him that Kerry might not know he was alone, and the two against three odds made him a little more careful than he would have been at three to one.

Shouting, Ben said, 'Charlie, stay over there! I think we've got 'em between us!'

Then he left his place and skirted quickly around in the darkness to a quartering position. He fired four fast rounds with his sixgun, and reloaded as someone near the corral corner answered him. The bullets, aimed in the vicinity of the muzzle flash, did no more harm than kick up snow.

Trying to deepen his voice, he yelled, 'Ben! Ben, try to get behind 'em!'

Two guns opened up from across the corral; he had them all counted now, all positioned, and they poured lead into the vicinity of Clayton's old position.

Ben almost laughed at the way they smoked up the place, thinking they were fighting two men. Still it wasn't so funny when he thought about it, for the responsibility of keeping the deception alive was his, and whipping those three wasn't a matter of playing games. Somehow, he had to lower the odds to two to one, and get away with it.

He began to Indian through the snow, flat on his belly, heading for the near corner of the corral where he'd last seen the lone muzzle flash. The yard was quiet and although the lights were still on in the house, nobody poked their nose out, and he was grateful for that.

It took him a few minutes to move toward the corral and he couldn't see a danged thing, so he stopped and thought it over. One thing for sure, he had some element of surprise in his favor, and he decided to be bold about it.

So he shouted, 'Charlie, I'm over here!'

Not ten yards away a man bounded over in the snow and flung a shot at Clayton. The bullet passed near and Ben swung his gun as the man shot again. A hook came out of nowhere and snatched Ben around, slamming him down in the snow, and his left arm went completely numb. Then he caught Al Manners rising and put the .45 bullet right dead center in his chest.

After Manners fell, Ben lay back in the snow and breathed heavily. He was hurt bad and he knew it, and he was afraid to take a look and see how bad.

There was no shooting from the other side of the corral, and Ben forced himself to a sitting position. He yelled, 'Charlie! Charlie, I got one!'

And immediately Joe Kerry began to call out. 'Al! Al, answer me!'

The silence was an answer in itself. Ben Clayton knew the yard was no good for him now. He was bleeding badly and his whole side felt numb, but that would wear off soon enough. Then he'd have the pain to fight.

Getting into the house was the only thing, and he started to belly across the yard, dragging his useless arm in the snow. He couldn't help think that more than likely he was going to die before dawn, and the prospect didn't frighten him as much as he thought it would. As for keeping up the ruse that Charlie Gannon was with him, Ben was willing to drop that now. He didn't need Charlie and he didn't want him. This time he was on his own, really out there by himself, and he didn't mind it; rather, he liked it and feared it and entertained a wonder of it at the same time.

He got around the corner of the house before Kerry and George Manners realized he was getting under cover.

'After him!' Kerry yelled. And they came plowing through the snow toward the house. With a new strength, Ben Clayton made it to his feet, banged on the door and spoke, and it opened.

Louise slammed it closed and shoved the bar in place, then her eyes went round and she gasped when she saw the blood running down his arm and off his fingers.

'Get me my rifle!' he gasped. 'Hurry!'

Louise just shook her head dumbly, and her mother said, 'I burned it.' She pointed to the blackened iron lying near the stove.

He looked at her for a moment, then said, 'Damn you people anyway!'

'You're hurt. I'll take care of it,' Mrs. Benson said. 'Reba, help me.'

'Keep away from me,' Clayton said. He turned to the lamp on the table and reduced the room to darkness with one shot. 'Board up those back windows.'

Kerry and George Manners were in position now; they scattered the glass in the front two windows and thudded bullets into the door. Ben Clayton let his knees go lax a minute and sat on the floor, his back to the wall. With the rifle gone, he had nothing now. Just the .45 which was no match at all against Winchesters.

'Ben?' The voice came from the darkness, Jenny Regan's voice; she fumbled for him, found him, and knelt beside him, her arms around him. He could feel the soft warmth of her through her nightgown, and he put his arm around her, to comfort her, or to find some measure of comfort for himself.

'I didn't know she burned the rifle, Ben.'

'It's all right,' he said. The pain was beginning to come now, the torn muscles and shattered nerves and fragmented bone all screaming out their individual tortures.

'It's not all right,' she said. 'How bad are you hurt?'

'My arm, it's busted for sure,' he said. Then he gave her a shove away from him. 'Go help the others, Jenny. We'll be here for a while.'

'Ben, I've got my shotgun under the bed. She never knew about it.'

'Get it,' he said.

She left him and he closed his eyes and tried not to be sick. It was no good, being inside the house. Kerry and George could pepper them as they pleased, and sooner or later they'd get someone in there.

And there was really only one defender, one gun, and he couldn't last long. They'd found the blood trail, he was sure. Just give it time, he thought, and I'll bleed out like a winged deer.

He'd pass out, or die then, and maybe Kerry and George wouldn't be satisfied with that, with the women around. Even in the darkness he could see Louise's face, in his mind, and he remembered George Manners and it was enough to tell him what he had to do.

The thought was new to Ben, dying for a woman who didn't love him, whose life was so far from his that they could barely reach each other. But he guessed that was what he'd do, die for her, because it was a manly thing, a role he felt compelled to play out.

Jenny came back with the shotgun and some brass shells. The women were nailing up the last pieces of wood over the windows; they'd ripped the table and beds apart to get it.

'Light another lamp,' Ben said softly, his breath whistling between his teeth.

A match sputtered and the chimney was set in place. Outside, the shooting stopped for a while, and Ben supposed the two men were puzzled as to why another lamp should have been lit.

He took the shotgun from Jenny, broke it open to check the loads, then put the loose shells in his coat pocket. Mrs. Benson was standing there, arms folded across her ample breasts. Ben Clayton smiled at her as he fumbled with his shell belt, laying the gun and holster on the floor.

'I'm going back out,' he said.

'You're a fool, young man,' Mrs. Benson

said.

He didn't get angry at her. 'What good are you besides moppin' floors and having kids?' He took Jenny Regan by the arm. 'Cover the lamp with a blanket. Louise, you open the door so I can get through.' He almost said a lot of stupid sentimental things but he choked these back. 'After I'm outside, you keep this door closed, you hear?'

'Don't go, Ben,' Jenny said.

He shook his head. 'The cold helps stop the bleeding.' Then he was sorry he'd said that. It had too much bravado in it; it was that danged bragging again. He just couldn't seem to get over it.

They smothered the lamp, bringing the room to instant darkness, and Louise opened the door. Then she knelt quickly, her arm going around his neck, and her lips clumsily slid along his cheek until they found his, then they clung there for an instant, warm and moist and promising even when she knew she had no right to promise anything.

He broke away and went through the door and it closed without slamming; he was glad they had enough sense not to tip Kerry off that he was not in the house.

The snow felt good and he lay in it for a moment to catch his breath and feel the tingle of his lips where Louise had kissed him. He supposed she'd carry through her life now a spot of sin for that bold forbidden thing. That was too bad, too, because it was a nice kiss; maybe they weren't so far apart as he'd first thought.

Behind the house was a rock jumble, and he didn't think Kerry or George would hole up there; there were no windows in back to shoot through. No, they'd be in front all right, out in the yard, belly flat and waiting for something to break, or thinking up some way to get in without being shot up.

Clayton thought about going after them, and knew it wouldn't work; he was running out of steam, and the pain was real bad now. This was one of those times when he did his thinking without fooling himself. The truth was there, staring him in the face: he had about an hour left, then he wouldn't have enough left in him to lift a finger and wave good-bye.

'So come to me, you sonsabitches,' Ben said softly.

Calling out to them, announcing himself, would be stupid; they had rifles and could lay down a lattice of lead around the house that was bound to get him. No, he had to think of something else, so he crawled close to the door and scratched on it like a dog trying to get in. He heard one of the women sob, then Jenny Regan spoke.

'Who's there?'

'It's me. Ben,' he said, his face pressed near the bottom crack. 'Jenny, listen to me. Jenny?'

'I'm right here, Ben.'

'I want you to open the door,' he said. 'Keep the lamp on, but don't get near the door. Just open it and stay against the wall. Jenny, can you hear me?'

'I can hear you.'

'I want them to come on in close enough for me to use this shotgun,' Clayton said. 'Now open it in three minutes, and keep back.'

'All right,' she said. 'Ben?'

'What?'

'I wish I could help you. I wish I had the strength to help you.'

'Open it in three minutes,' he said, and bellied away.

He took a station to one side of the door, where the night was deep and he could not be seen. And he held the shotgun steady with his right hand, the butt against his stomach. The shells in his pocket were next to worthless to him, because he'd have to put the gun down to reach for them. There wouldn't be time for that after the shooting started.

Two shots, that's what he had, one barrel for George, and the other for Joe Kerry.

The door opened slowly, like someone letting in fresh air. There was no sound at all from inside the house, and a shaft of yellow lamplight fell on the snow. Ben Clayton reached out and covered his legs with snow to make himself even less visible, and waited.

He was surprised when crying came from inside the house; the women were setting up a

187

regular wailing wall in there, he guessed, from the sound of it, and for a minute he didn't figure it at all. Then he understood what they were doing. They were crying for a dead man, a man who had died trying to protect them. Crying because they were now helpless and afraid. He wondered whose idea that had been. Jenny's probably. It was hard to frighten her so bad she couldn't think.

Then he saw the two dark shapes rise from the snow in the yard and come forward cautiously, rifles cocked and ready. They were a good forty yards out and he had a hard time holding his trigger finger slack; they were that tempting a target.

As they drew nearer, Kerry waved George away from him and the two men split, approaching the door ninety degrees apart from each other. This presented a problem to Ben Clayton. George Manners was coming straight on, which wasn't so bad, but once he cut loose with the shotgun, Kerry would start firing, or duck for cover.

So he'd have to move fast, and the thought was in his mind that maybe he couldn't with the arm hindering him. Any movement was now pure misery and made him sick.

For George Manners, Clayton set the range for fifteen yards; that would put Kerry, on the other side, at about thirty, a little long for quick buckshot scattering, but it had to be that way.

He counted the steps Manners took, and when it was just right, Ben gave in to one more boastful impulse, and said, 'Good-bye, George.'

He fired on the heels of it, watched Manners snatched off his feet, then turned the shotgun on Joe Kerry. Kerry's rifle cracked and the bullet slivered the wall over Ben Clayton's head, then he pulled the trigger, discharging his last barrel.

The shot scattered a little wider than he figured it would, but a few of the .36 caliber pellets got Kerry somewhere in the legs, for he spun around and went down. But he wasn't down for good. He tried to lever his rifle as Ben broke open the shotgun to reload, but as he fumbled for the shells, he knew he wasn't going to make it.

Kerry was sitting up, shouldering his rifle and Ben kept thinking, don't cry out but take it like a man. Then the doorway darkened and Mrs. Benson stepped out; she had Ben's .45 Colt and she sighted carefully. The gun recoiled in her hand and Joe Kerry flipped over backward in the snow, flopped his arms about for an instant, then lay still.

Lowering the gun, Mrs. Benson said, 'Young man, where are you?'

Clayton said something, made some noise, because Mrs. Benson called to the others. 'Louise, Reba, Ellen—help him up.'

Their hands lifted him and he nearly fainted

from the pain in him. Mrs. Benson's face was stern, her manner blunt. 'Be easy there! He's not a bag of oats!' When they carried him through the door, he looked at her and tried a small smile.

Her expression didn't change. She said, 'I can do other things besides mop and have kids, young man.'

He nodded his head weakly. 'You've got a sin—now,' he said.

'It isn't my first,' she admitted. 'And I'll live with it.' She went ahead and into Jenny Regan's bedroom. Jenny was there, and she put out her hand to Clayton's forehead when they put him on the bed. Louise quickly pushed her hand away.

'I'll do that,' she said tartly.

'Get some light in here, and a pair of scissors and hot water,' Mrs. Benson said. Ben sank back on the soft bed and listened to her give orders like a sergeant major; that woman didn't let down for a minute.

His mind was a fog of pain and he kept twisting his head from side to side, trying not to cry out. Mrs. Benson came in and put the lamp on the table. She looked at him, then said, 'Swear if it hurts, young man. It's no sin to cry.'

She directed Louise to cut away the bloody coat sleeve and the shirt, and they stripped him to the waist, which embarrassed him more than anything he'd ever known. Tears ran down

Louise's face and she kept brushing at them angrily.

Then her mother said, 'Do you want this man, child?' She didn't say anything, just nodded, and Mrs. Benson snorted. 'He's not your kind, Louise. Only hurt will come of it.'

The girl turned to her mother then, her expression angry, her voice angry. 'There's all kinds of men, Ma, and they're not all bad!'

'You can't work when you're crying,' Mrs. Benson said, elbowing her aside. She knelt by the bed and looked at Ben Clayton's arm, and her expression turned grim, and she had to bite her lip to keep her own feelings back. Gently she wiped the sweat from Clayton's forehead. She said, 'It took a man to stand out there tonight with the blood of life running out of him, Ben. But there's one thing hard about being that kind of a man. You have to go on being that way. Ben, do you hear me?'

'Yeah,' he said, breathing heavily. 'What are you saying?'

Her voice turned gentle as the wind, and the stern discipline left her face, and it became plump and soft and full of tenderness. 'Ben, will you look at your arm?'

It seemed that he didn't want to, but he forced himself. The bullet had caught him just below the elbow and had made a ruin of the bone and joint. He looked at it, then closed his eyes and said, 'God! It's bad.'

'Yes, it's real bad, Ben. I don't think the best

doctor in the world could do anything for it.'
She patted his face and stroked his damp hair.
'Ben, a real man can hold a woman with one
arm. You see that, don't you? He could if he
was a real man; it wouldn't make him feel less.'

He shook his head. 'I can't bear—to think of
it.'

'You've got to. You didn't want to die out
there. Why should you want to die now? Life is
long, Ben. There's a sweetness to it a body
never tires of. It's got to come off, Ben.'

'When?' he asked.

'The morning will be soon enough,' she said.
'Louise will stay with you, now, and I guess
always.'

Then she got up and motioned the rest of
them out of the room, except Louise, and
closed the door. She was not a woman who
cried, but she fought back the tears with little
effect.

Jenny Regan watched her, then said, 'Can
you take off his arm, Mrs. Benson?'

'I must,' she said. 'Or he'll die.'

CHAPTER TWELVE

After eight days of southward movement,
Charlie Gannon began to think he was being
led on a long, hopeless chase. Then he
detected a gradually enlarging alertness among

the Indians. In their evening camps they began to talk less to themselves and listen more attentively to the small night sounds.

They were in the Apache country all right, Gannon knew, and it was a constant crawling feeling down the middle of his back. He always cooked his own meals, and he was brewing up a pot of coffee when he became aware that their number had increased.

He looked up at the penny-shaded face at the edge of the fire and then turned his head to find four others there, behind him and to each side. Then he went back to brewing his coffee, as though he'd expected them all along.

'The man is not afraid,' one of the Apaches said, stepping forward. He was tall and slender, a magnificent man. 'I am Diablito. You have a name?'

'Gannon.' He made a motion for him to sit. 'Coffee?'

The Apache hesitated, then gathered his blanket about him and squatted across the fire. He carried a brass-receivered Henry rifle, and leaned this against his thigh to accept the cup.

'Why do you come here?' Diablito asked.

'I want the boy,' Gannon said. 'The one Shanti has.' He looked at the Indian steadily. 'I know Shanti is here.'

'You know this,' Diablito said, 'because the brother of Shanti is a woman!'

Immediately there was an argument but Diablito could curse longer and shout louder than the others, so they shut up and sat with sullen faces. Gannon didn't understand any of it but he could make a pretty good guess at the gist of it. Diablito was sore because the Piutes had led a white man into their stronghold, a touchy place for any man to be. From the way Diablito spoke English, Gannon guessed that he'd gone to school at the San Carlos reservation, but it hadn't bred the danger out of him, or the savagery either.

'I need no words from them to tell me what I know,' Gannon said flatly.

Shanti's brother went into a voluble account of the 'glass' Gannon had, and Diablito listened to this with growing disgust. Gannon didn't like the look on his face at all, and he liked it a lot less when Diablito turned to him to speak.

'I will see this medicine.'

'It's in my saddlebag,' Gannon said, acting as though it didn't matter whether he saw it or not.

An Apache brought it to Diablito who examined it briefly, then laughed and broke it to pieces on a rock. Again he went into a long cursing tirade against Indian stupidity, only this time the Piutes just packed up and left the camp.

Gannon didn't let anything show on his face, but worry loomed large in his mind. 'Where are they going?' he asked.

'To their land,' Diablito said. 'I am not a

fool, white man. The glass I can buy in the trading post for three dollars. It has no power.'

Gannon smiled behind his beard stubble. 'It got me here, didn't it?'

'But it will not get you out,' Diablito stated. 'Come. We go now.'

'Go where?'

They weren't the arguing kind. An Apache rapped Gannon on the back of the head with a rifle butt, just enough to stun him and knock him down. He rolled over and looked at them.

Diablito said, 'To your feet. I am in a hurry, and because of that I will allow you to ride. Otherwise you would walk with a rope around your neck.'

'It makes sense,' Gannon said and got up. His head hurt like blazes, but he didn't bother to rub it; all these Apaches were sensitive about a man's courage, his ability to take it. So as long as he could keep the rough knocks to himself, the fear inside, where it didn't show, he had a better than average chance of bluffing his way through.

The fire was put out and he mounted up, after the Apaches had taken his rifle and shells. These were valuable items to a warlike people.

He rode in the middle and made no overt move, or gave them cause not to trust him, believing in the old saw that you could catch more flies with honey than you could with vinegar.

The Apaches believed in moving along, and they knew all the dark trails. It was almost dawn before they reached the main camp. It was just like the Piutes', dirty, full of foul odor and noisy dogs.

He expected the camp to be bigger, but then he remembered things he'd been told, about how the Apaches never gathered more than fifteen or twenty in one camp. They couldn't conform to a social order like the Sioux or Comanches.

Gannon could see that they were poor, for they weren't hunters, just thieves, and stealing had been thin, with army posts here and there and everyone taking a shoot-first, ask-questions-afterward attitude.

Every man in the camp came forward to see the prisoner, to look at him and figure out what they could use in the way of his clothing after he had no more use for them. Some of the Apaches wore bits of cavalry uniform, and one wore the top of a woman's dress; the bottom had been cut off and given to a favorite squaw.

Diablito was second in command here; an ancient, withered gnome was in charge. He looked at Gannon for a moment, then motioned for him to sit by the fire.

'He is Cuchillo Pedro, my father,' Diablito said. 'He does not speak your tongue, so I will tell you what he says.'

'Just make sure you get it right,' Gannon

said dryly. 'It wouldn't do to have more misunderstandin' than there is already.' He took out his sack of tobacco and calmly rolled a smoke, and all the time Cuchillo Pedro watched him intently.

Then the old man spoke, and when he was through, Diablito put the question in English. 'He wants to know why you are here?'

Gannon glanced at him, then said, 'Tell him I'm here because a thievin' Piute stole my boy, and I want him back.' He puffed on his cigaret. 'Tell him I want him back now.'

This was done, and the old man had a lot to say about it.

'My father says that he has bought the boy.'

Gannon thought about this, wondering if it were the truth or not. Then he said, 'Where's Shanti?'

'He has gone back to his people.'

'You're a liar,' Gannon said. He expected to be belted for that, but Diablito only compressed his lips and grew grim in the eyes. 'You wouldn't let him go, so don't tell me different. Ask him what he paid for the boy.'

Diablito asked the question, and translated. 'My father took him as a gift.'

'Where's Shanti?'

'I have said—'

'You've told me a pack of lies!' Gannon flared. 'He came here with the boy because he was afraid. And he wouldn't go back now. I want to see the boy.'

197

'He is not here,' Diablito said.

Gannon nodded as though he believed this lie, then he began to yell. 'Beans! Beans!'

And he heard the boy answer, from one of the *jacals*, but that was all for he was struck heavily on the head with a rifle butt. Gannon fell forward to let blackness cover him. Diablito reached out and with his foot turned Gannon away from the fire.

Cuchillo Pedro spoke softly to his son. 'This man is brave. Bring Shanti to the fire.' He waited with an ancient patience, and when Shanti came from one of the *jacals*, he paused before facing the Piute leader.

'When I took the boy,' Cuchillo Pedro said, 'you told me the parents were dead. I do not like lies, Shanti. The true friends of Cuchillo Pedro do not lie to him as you have lied.'

'I did not believe he would come this far,' Shanti said hurriedly.

'The harm is done,' Cuchillo Pedro said. 'If he could find us, the soldiers will also find us. It is on your head, Shanti, not mine.' He made a sweeping motion with his hand. 'Tomorrow you will take the boy and the man and go. Go far from my land. Let the soldiers hang *you*.'

'How can I go back to my people?' Shanti asked. 'If the white man had not given us the whiskey, I would be warm in my lodge, with honor among my people. Can Shanti be held to blame for what the white man has done?'

'I do not choose to decide,' Cuchillo Pedro

said flatly. 'Go, Shanti. Take this man and the boy with you.'

'The man is my enemy,' Shanti pleaded. 'He has followed me this far, across many mountains. He would strike death to me if the chance were his.'

'A wise man strikes death to his enemies before it is too late,' Cuchillo Pedro said. 'Shanti, I will advise you. Take the boy and the man into the mountains. When you come out, be alone.'

'Kill the boy? He is like my son who is long dead.'

Cuchillo Pedro shook his head sadly. 'It is a thing you are not meant to have, Shanti.' He waved his hand once and the talk was ended.

When Gannon came to, he found himself bound hand and foot, face down on the cold ground, without so much as an old blanket to cover him. The back of his head was a solid ache and he knew there was an egg-sized lump there.

How long he'd been out was a mystery to him, but the camp was quiet. Only one guard walked up and down by the fire, and Gannon wished he were a little closer to it. The chills ran all the way through him and he was past the stage of shivering. The ropes around his ankles and wrists cut off his circulation and he had no feeling at all in his feet or hands.

The guard looked at him once or twice but Gannon made no move at all, and after a while the guard stopped bothering and just walked up and down. For a time Gannon silently cursed the Apaches for binding him with rawhide and not rope; a man could more often than not work a rope free, but not rawhide. The more it dried the tighter it pulled, and unless it was wet there wasn't any stretch to it at all.

His hands were bound, and his feet and his legs drawn up behind him. It was a hell of a position for a man to be in. Getting loose was his first thought; he could work the rest out as soon as his hands and feet were free.

The hands came first and he twisted them brutally against the rawhide binding and clenched his teeth against the pain of it. He could feel no relaxing, no stretching of the lashings, and took a deep breath and tried it again. He knew he brought blood to the surface that time; he could feel it make his wrists slick. He lay motionless for a time, trying not to breathe hard and attract the guard's attention. Then, when the Apache's back was turned or he walked to the far edge of camp, Gannon twisted and strained at the rawhide and thought he felt some give.

The blood was doing it, he guessed, soaking, softening the rawhide, and he waited a bit, to let the bindings soften and to let the pain in his arms die off a little. Gannon didn't need a blanket now, for he was sweating, and he buried his face in the snow to cool it.

200

Slowly the rawhide stretched until by bunching his fingers and thumbs together, Gannon could work it down over the backs of his hands. He had no way to measure the passage of time but he figured it must have taken him an hour to do this, for he had to work carefully and not attract the guard.

And when his hands were free, he still couldn't straighten his legs to ease the cramps in them. He could, but he didn't dare. Then he started to work on the rawhide thongs around his ankles, and instead of being easy, it proved more difficult than freeing his wrists. The blood made his fingers slippery, and the cold built a clumsiness into his hands that he had never known before.

Then the circulation started to come back, and a pain so sharp, so intense that he almost fainted just trying to keep it inside him. His fingers turned to flame, were consumed one by one by fire, and he had to endure it all without an outcry.

Back and forth walked the Apache guard, unaware of the agony.

And Gannon's life depended on him remaining unaware.

The circulation came back, and the pain died away, but the cuts on his wrists burned now. He could ignore that, though, for it was a good hurt, the kind a man felt in his back and kidneys after breaking a particularly mean and dangerous horse.

By the time he got back to work on the ankle knots, the blood had dried on his fingers and rawhide, and this time he had more success. With the bindings free, he had to force himself to lie there and endure it all again, the shooting pains in his legs, each toe a kernel of agony.

Straightening his legs all the way would have helped, but he dared not do that; he still had to remain in a tied posture or the guard would see that something was wrong. Still, he could lower his legs somewhat, a little at a time, so that the difference wouldn't be readily noticed.

Gannon wasn't sure he could get up and run if he had the chance, but he knew he couldn't lie much longer. He was free now and had to make his break.

Feeling around behind him, he thrust his hands into the snow and found a small rock. When the Apache's back was turned, Gannon lobbed this toward the other end of the camp, and when the guard heard it hit, he went to investigate. He was gone some minutes, then he came back, not satisfied with his search, but very alert. Which was just what Gannon wanted.

He sorted around again, found a stone the size of his fist, and put it to one side, where he could get to it quickly. Then he found another smaller one, waited his chance, and threw it. This time the Apache examined the perimeter of the camp more thoroughly, and when he came back, he looked long at Gannon, who lay motionless, hands and feet behind him, apparently asleep.

With eyes pulled nearly closed, Gannon watched him, and then the Indian came over and bent down to examine him, to feel if his bindings were secure. Gannon caught him that way, off guard, and smashed the rock against the Apache's temple. From the hollow, broken sound of the blow, Gannon knew that he had killed him. Almost as the Indian fell, Gannon grabbed the Henry rifle and belt of shells.

When he tried to stand, he fell, and had to move along on his hands and knees until he finally reached the edge of the camp. There he paused to think, to consider his next move. He'd come for the boy and he wasn't leaving without him, although each minute of hesitation magnified the risks. Anything could happen now. An Apache could come out of a *jacal* just to find out what kind of a morning it was going to be, see the dead guard and arouse the camp, and he wouldn't have a chance.

Every instinct told him to get out, now, while there was time. It was a difficult thing to resist, this temptation to save himself and let the boy go. What was he anyway, but some kid they'd taken in out of goodness of the heart; he really wasn't hers, and it wasn't the same as if he'd been hers. He wouldn't even have to tell her how it was, how there was only time for one to make it; there was no need for her to

203

know those details. He could just say that he hadn't found the boy at all, or that he had and that he was dead. It would be a cruel thing for Jenny, but she would get over it. She'd have him, a man who loved her enough to make the hurt go away.

It was his life or the boy's and the measuring of them was not easy. He thought then that he'd better not say that the boy was dead. Someday, by some miracle, he might just pop up unexpectedly, and Gannon didn't want to be caught in a lie like that.

The baseness of this calculation stunned him, left him feeling indescribably dirty, and he put his face in his hands and considered the kind of man he must be, and knew he would never be the same again. He would never be able to accept Jenny's love or live his life with this hidden in his mind, a smudge on his soul. It would be better, he decided, to die here with the boy than to live on his own miserable terms. With him dead, she might find happiness with some decent man.

He could not figure out which *jacal* housed the boy; that one brief answering cry gave him no direction before the Apache hit him with the rifle. But he was in the camp, close by, and yet impossibly far away.

The fire was dying out, and he watched it for a moment, then left his cover and braved the dangers of returning to the center of the camp. Picking up a few burning fagots, Gannon ran around to the rear of three *jacals* and got them blazing, then crossed over to the other side so he wouldn't have the fires at his back.

They caught quickly, and were burning fiercely before the alarmed cry went out. The Apaches vacated their burning shelters quickly, and the others ran out, too, to keep the flying embers from catching.

Gannon saw Shanti come out. He was holding the boy's hand tightly, and Gannon ducked back, swung around the *jacal*, and came up behind Shanti. He would have made it a complete surprise had not Beans caught sight of him, and because he was a child, he yelled Gannon's name.

Shanti turned and Gannon did what he had to do, what he didn't want to do. He shot the old man in the head, grabbed the boy and tried to make a run for it. The shot told the Apaches everything, that their prisoner had killed the guard, fired the *jacals* and was now trying to escape.

Diablito organized the search party, four young braves who quickly grabbed their rifles and followed him from camp. Gannon and the boy ran, and when the boy couldn't keep up Gannon scooped him up and carried him. But running was a product of his fear, his desperation, and that faded and he began to think.

If they kept on running, they'd both be dead within the hour. To live, he'd have to use his brains and out-smart them. So he went into the rocks where the wind had blown the snow clear, and he began to climb, feeling his way along, making sure he left no sign.

Daylight wouldn't be long in coming, a couple of hours or so; that didn't give him much time at all. And he was tired, all the way through to the core of his bones. There wasn't much left in him, just the will to go on, the will to make his legs do what he wanted them to do, push him ever higher toward the rocky ridge.

He had no plan of escape, just survival. To escape he'd need a horse. The Apaches knew that, and would be guarding them closely. Gannon figured it would take Diablito all of ten minutes to pick up the trail; there weren't any better at the business of man hunting.

Gannon was forced to rest, and he sat on a rock.

'Put me down,' Beans said. 'I want down.'

He hadn't realized that he was still holding the boy, and he set him on his feet. Shanti or someone had given him an old blanket to wear, a filthy wraparound, and the boy shivered from the cold.

'Don't talk,' Gannon said. The Apaches had sharp ears and on a still night like this, a voice, even a soft one, would carry a great distance. The hard rock felt good. Just sitting felt good, but it couldn't last. He took the boy by the hand and started to climb again.

When they broke out on the crest of the ridge, Gannon fell to the ground and lay there, breathing heavily through his open mouth. Somewhere below, but following, were the Apaches, and he cursed this weakness in him that kept him from going on.

There was a notion in his mind to just hole up and fight it out. He had the rifle and some shells. Then he told himself that this was the most stupid idea yet. The Apaches would surround him and just starve him out. And the four who followed him weren't the only Apaches near; the number might swell to twelve before noontime came around.

The only advantage he could see to making a stand of it would be that he would die rested. And it was a shame, too, that he'd spent all that energy climbing to the ridge, since now he knew that the only way out was to go back, get into the Apache camp, and try to overpower the horse guard.

He did not go down the way he had come up, and he took care to stay on bare ground. They moved carefully and paused often to listen. When Gannon heard a slight sound off to his left somewhere he grew very quiet. The boy held his hands and trembled.

There was a low guttural murmur of talk, then the Apaches passed on, still climbing for the ridge. Gannon guessed it would take them another fifteen minutes to get to the top and decide he'd gone back down. It was uncanny the way they'd picked up his trail in the dark, but there was no time to figure it out; they knew their business, which was bad for Gannon.

The *jacals* he'd set afire were now ashes and a few flying sparks. Aside from the women and children milling around, the Apache camp seemed deserted; all the men, except the ones guarding the horses, were out hunting. He counted two, one near him, the other on the far side. That was bad, but after odds which a minute ago had seemed terrible, two against one was suddenly very good.

He picked out the horse he wanted, a rangy bay, then leveled his rifle and killed the Apache nearest him. The shot would bring the others down off the ridge in one big hurry; already the other guard was moving to one side, so he could get a clean shot at Gannon.

Scooping up Beans, he flung him astride the horse, and went up after him. The remaining horse guard snapped a shot at Gannon, and missed, and Gannon didn't give him a chance to shoot again. He whooped and drove the horses into a frightened run right over the Apache, and when Gannon and the boy cleared camp, he didn't look back to see whether he was alive or not.

The Apaches were afoot and he was mounted; he had his start now, a good one, and for the first time since he'd entered the country he entertained a genuine hope of getting out. And with what he'd come after. It was humiliating to think now of ever having considered leaving Beans behind.

Gannon made a fast, wild ride of it, making a circle to again move northward and out of the country. In the morning there'd be smoke on the high peaks, and soon every Apache in the territory would be looking for them. But he didn't give a damn about the dawn, or the odds now. He was out of death's immediate reach and he had the boy, and the feel of his small strong hands around his waist was a good thing.

The horse grew tired and Gannon had to stop. He picked a small rocky pocket for their day camp. Beans slid off and Gannon sat there for a moment, trying to remember the source of his hammering headache.

Then he said, 'Take my rifle, boy.'

Beans stood there, his innocent eyes wide and puzzled. 'What rifle?'

Charlie Gannon thought he misunderstood the boy, or was it the other way around? He said, 'Take the rifle so I can get down.'

'You don't got it,' Beans said.

Gannon looked at his hand, his left hand, and couldn't quite make it out. It was half closed, as though it had been holding something, but had long ago dropped it and forgotten to relax. In the faint dawn light, the dried blood made it look black, like a muddy chicken foot, and he stopped looking at it.

He slid off the horse and felt his legs give like two pieces of oiled leather. The ground came up hard and suddenly he lay there. Beans grabbed the reins and held them to keep the horse from bolting.

'Good boy,' Gannon said. 'I'll be all right—after I rest a while.'

It made the boy feel good, comfortable, protected; he could tell by his expression, and Charlie Gannon was glad he could fool him. It might be easier that way. But he couldn't fool himself, not when he thought of the miles ahead.

But the only part about dying that really hurt him was the knowledge that the boy would die too.

CHAPTER THIRTEEN

Captain Anders was not a man who liked to give up on a thing. Neither was he a man who pursued foolishly when turning back followed every reason of logic. Which was why he swung his detail about and went back to Jenny Regan's place, arriving shortly after the first blush of a gray dawn.

Sergeant Brusso and his men were already there, having arrived a bit earlier, and as Anders dismounted, he could see an unusual worry on Brusso's face.

The sergeant met him as Anders approached the door. 'I'm sure glad to see you back, sir,' Brusso said. He pointed to three blanket-covered men just around the corner of the house. 'That's Kerry and the Manners boys. Clayton fought it out with 'em sometime last night.'

'Is he dead?' Anders asked quickly.

'You'd better come in the house, sir.' He went ahead and opened the door for Anders.

Jenny Regan was sitting on a box and she got up as soon as Anders came in. 'Mrs. Benson! Mrs. Benson, Captain Anders came back!'

The bedroom door opened and Mrs. Benson came out. 'Do you know how to amputate a man's arm, Captain?'

'What?' He brushed past her and went into the bedroom where Ben Clayton lay gray and drawn, his eyes glazed by pain. Ander's voice was gentle. 'Looks like you caught one, Ben. Let me have a look at that.' He made his examination, frowning and clucking softly to himself. Then he turned and found Mrs. Benson and Jenny Regan standing in the doorway. 'Would one of you tell Sergeant Brusso to bring me the surgical kit?' He smiled at Ben Clayton. 'The army can't afford to send a surgeon on every patrol, but after fourteen years I've learned to patch up quite a variety of wounds.'

Mrs Benson. turned and went out, and Jenny

Regan came into the room. She took a blanket from the bureau drawer and spread it on the other side of the bed. Anders frowned and raised up, then saw Louise Benson sleeping there.

'She was with him all night,' Jenny said. 'It wasn't easy.'

Louise stirred and groaned and finally sat up. Her eyes were puffed and red and Anders couldn't rightly tell whether it was from weariness or grief. She started when he spoke to her. 'You'd better go on out. We'll take care of him now.'

She started to turn to Ben Clayton to say something, but Sergeant Brusso came in bearing a heavy leather case. 'Where do you want me to set this, sir?'

'On that chair will do,' Anders said. 'We could stand some more heat in here now.'

'Mrs. Benson thought the cold would help stop the bleeding,' Jenny said.

'It did. But now we've got to patch this tomcat up. Bring in a pail of coals from the stove, and set it in the middle of the floor.' Then he turned to the surgical case and opened it. 'I'm probably the worst doctor you ever saw, Ben, but I've got something here that'll kill that pain.' He prepared a needle, filling it carefully, then sank it into the muscle of Clayton's shoulder. 'You tell me when you begin to feel a little better.'

He dared not speak for fear of crying out, so

212

he only nodded at Anders. The captain sat there a few minutes, patiently waiting. He watched the pupils of Ben Clayton's eyes, and the glassiness began to leave them.

Finally Clayton sighed and said, 'Oh, that's good.'

'The pain will go away after a while,' Anders said. 'That was laudanum. I've got some other stuff here too.' He pulled away the loose wrappings on Clayton's arm and examined it more critically. The light was steadily getting better as the dawn flushed full.

Louise came in with a pail of red coals and the heat began to drive back the chill. Anders looked at her, then said, 'I can use some help. Do you want to?'

'Anything,' she said softly, gratefully.

Anders didn't miss this, but there was no time to think about it. 'About the only reason you haven't bled to death, Ben, is that the main arteries are intact. A lot of tissue destruction and bone damage, but the artery is unpunctured.' He scratched his beard stubble, then got out the handbook and read for a few minutes. He closed it with a snap and held it in his hands while he leaned forward to speak. 'Ben, I can take off the arm and you'll never feel it. But if I do that, I'll be getting into something I don't know much about, like tying off that artery. And you've lost so damned much blood now that you're white as a sheet. If you bleed much more, I couldn't help you.'

213

'What's on your mind, Doc?'

Anders thought a bit. 'Well, either way as I see it, you've got a bad arm there. If it comes off, you're crippled. If it don't come off, you'll never bend that elbow a quarter of an inch for the rest of your life. The joint, or what's left of it, may just heal solid. And likely it'll give you fits when the weather changes. Or the arm may be two, three inches shorter than the other.'

'Would I be able to use the fingers?' Clayton asked.

Anders shrugged. 'Ben, I couldn't guarantee a thing.'

'Well, that's the way I wanted to hear it,' Ben Clayton said. He took Louise Benson's hand and held it. 'That laud—anum stuff is working fine; the pain's about gone.'

'Good,' Anders said. 'We've got some new medicine they're handing out in bottles, although the damned stuff evaporates like blazes. I'm going to put a cloth over your nose, Ben, and you just breathe deeply. While you're under I'm going to try to take tweezers and pick out all the bone splinters and clean up that arm. If it gets infected, it'll have to come off.'

He got his tools ready and placed the wad of cloth over Clayton's nose. Then he handed the bottle of ether to Louise Benson. 'Just pour a little on the cloth, and watch him. If he groans, pour a little more. Have you got that?'

'Yes,' she said.

214

The women crowded through the door while Anders worked. He had a time cleaning the wound, getting all those slivers of exploded bone and lead, and Louise never took her glance off Ben Clayton, now and then adding a little ether when a small moan escaped him.

When Anders began to bandage, he talked while he worked. 'If you've ever had a broken bone, you'll know that it was always held in place with wooden splints. Well, they've got something new now.' He took several rolls of gauzy bandages from the chest and a paper sack full of white powder. At his request, one of the Benson women brought in a pan of hot water and Anders bandaged the arm from the wrist nearly to the elbow. He also went above the wound and bandaged to Clayton's shoulder. Then he mixed up the paste and covered the gauze. 'When that dries,' Anders said, 'It'll be like adobe. Strong, too.'

Sergeant Brusso went outside and found him some heavy wire, and around the shattered elbow, Anders built a cage, open at the top, and with gauze and plaster he made a protective knob, a cup in which the elbow rested, safe from harm, yet open for examination and drainage.

'Just like the pictures in the book, sir,' Brusso said.

'Yes, it is at that,' Anders said. 'A beautiful piece of work, if I do say so myself. It almost makes a man wish he had a broken arm,

215

doesn't it?'

'Well, not quite,' Brusso admitted. Then he frowned. 'How come you bent the elbow like that, sir?'

'Well, a man wouldn't want it to grow straight like a broom handle,' Anders said. 'Maybe he will be able to use the fingers, and if he can, a ninety-degree bend may come in handy for riding and a lot of things.' He slapped his thighs and got up. His hands were covered with dried and cracked plaster and he went outside to clean them off.

'Will he sleep without pain now?' Mrs. Benson asked.

Brusso shrugged. 'It'll be a while before that stuff wears off, ma'am. You know, I think the captain is a disappointed medical student. He sure likes to patch people up. You want to see my shoulder where the—'

'Some other time,' Mrs. Benson said quickly. 'Come, ladies, let's fix some hot food for the soldiers. You tell your men, Sergeant, that they'll be served in an hour.'

'That's an awful lot of work to—'

'A tub of beans is no more trouble than a pot of the same,' she said. 'You run the army. I'll run the kitchen.'

'Yes'm,' Brusso said and began to put the things back in the case.

Jenny Regan waited until the others went out, then she spoke to Brusso. 'What about Charlie? Why did Anders turn back?'

'I guess he lost him completely,' Brusso said. 'Jenny, if there had been any chance of picking up Gannon's trail the captain would have followed it through. You know that.'

She nodded. 'Yes, of course I know it.'

Brusso smiled and tried to ease her mind that way. 'You've got a couple of real tough boys here, Jenny. They don't know when to back off at all.' He shook his head in admiration. 'I'd have never tackled Joe Kerry and the Manners boys that way.' A frown came to his face, heavy and thick creasing across his blunt forehead. 'I guess it's my fault Clayton's layin' there with a shattered arm. All I was thinking of was making a hunk of bait of him to draw the Kerry bunch into the open. How did I know they'd break from the hills at sundown?' He got up and fastened the straps on the surgical case. 'I'd better tell the captain. He might want to do something.'

'Why tell him at all, Sergeant?'

He looked at her steadily for a moment, then shook his head. 'There's nothing between me and the captain. If I lose my stripes, then I've got it coming.'

Jenny said, 'It won't help you, or Ben, or Captain Anders. Why burn the barn down because the cow got out?' She touched him on the arm. 'Do we have to enumerate each little sin in our lives? Is it really better to confess?'

'It's funny you'd say that,' Brusso said. 'It sure is.'

217

'Why, because I read the Bible? Do you think Mrs. Benson is going to Hell because she shot Joe Kerry?'

Brusso laughed. 'The colonel's liable to pin a medal on her.' Then his humor faded. 'I see your point. We live with what we are, huh?'

'Or what we think we are,' Jenny said. 'Sergeant, we blame ourselves for a lot of things. Charlie Gannon is somewhere; I don't even know where. And I keep praying he'll come back to me, and I keep thinking that I'm not praying hard enough or he would come back. God forgive me, but I've even prayed that he'd come back without the boy, if only he'd just come back. Who do I confess that to?'

'To me,' Brusso said.

'But not to Charlie Gannon,' Jenny said. Then she turned and went into the kitchen to do what she could to help with breakfast.

*   *   *

Sometime during the day, when sleep was next to unconsciousness, Beans had gone into Gannon's pockets, found his tin of matches, then gathered brush and built a fire. The warmth of it brought Charlie Gannon back to a state of soothed awareness, then he sat up and blinked his eyes.

'I got cold,' Beans said simply.

The sight of the fire, the warmth of it, the sheer horror of it, knowing that for untold

218

hours it had been sending telltale smoke skyward, shocked Charlie Gannon immeasurably. His first impulse was to kick the fire to pieces, destroy it, but he knew how useless that was. The smoke had been seen, their positions marked in the minds of savage men who knew every rocky pass and hiding place within a hundred miles.

Well, what did it matter? This was Gannon's thought. They didn't have much of a chance anyway. He was close to the end of his string, with his fingers so stiff he couldn't close them. His wrists hurt and he tried not to move them and start the bleeding again.

Losing that rifle had been a tragedy, but he just could not believe it had slipped unnoticed from his numb fingers. All along he could feel the weight of it, the solidness of it, but it must have been in his mind. A fatal betrayal of the mind.

'I'm hungry,' Beans said. 'You hungry?' He crowded closer to the fire. 'I'm warm now. Are you warm?'

'Yes, I'm fine,' Gannon said. 'Are you all right, Beans?'

The boy gave him a quick smile. His face hadn't been washed once since he'd been taken, or his hands either, but he was happy the way he was. 'Do your hands hurt, Charlie?'

'Naw, they don't hurt,' Gannon said. 'What do you say we ride on? You want to see your mum, don't you?'

'Sure. I'll bet she's mad at me.'

'She won't be mad,' Gannon said. He was clumsy catching up the horse and clumsy mounting, and Beans had to stand on a rock to get on. If he ever fell off, Gannon thought, I wouldn't be able to help him on again.

'Have we got far to go?' Beans asked.

'Not far,' Gannon lied. 'We'll be home before you know it.'

'Will the pony be there when I get there?'

'He could be,' Gannon said and left the rocky pocket.

There was no way for him to know where the Apaches lay. He didn't even know where he was, and a town could have been hidden over the next ridge for all he knew. Keep going, that was his thought, and his direction was north and out of this *Apacheria*.

He considered himself lucky to travel out what was left of the day without seeing anyone, or being seen. And just before dark he rode down out of the hills and entered a long valley floor. The snow there was going to leave some clear enough tracks, but he was thinking of the distance he could travel on level ground, not the clarity of sign he left behind. As far as he could figure, it didn't make much difference one way or another; the Apaches could track him anyway.

It was too bad he didn't have blankets so the boy could sleep; he fretted a lot in the cold. And the wrappings he wore over his feet were playing out, so Gannon ripped up the lining of his coat and told Beans to use that.

There were just things a man had to do with his hands, hurt or not, and Gannon made himself flex the fingers and work the stiff wrists. They were swollen and sore from the struggle with the rawhide thongs, but he expected that would go down in a few days.

It wasn't a good feeling to be out in that wild country without a gun. He could hear cats screaming now and then, downing some animal or another. Cats or Apaches, he could never be sure. They were good at calling to each other with imitations.

He would have kept on going, but the boy just couldn't take an all-night ride and Gannon was forced to stop so he could rest. They found some shelter, and he decided to risk another fire. The boy curled up to it and went to sleep while Gannon dozed, sitting up.

Roast one side, and freeze the other; that's the way it was with him. A wind came up and promised to turn into a howler; it was all he needed now, one good snowstorm on top of the Apaches. Then he began to look on the other side of it. If the wind blew away their tracks, they could stay in the valleys where the going was better and, with luck, make thirty or forty miles a day.

But not without something to eat. Gannon's stomach was a solid empty ache, and he knew the boy was suffering, which was probably why he whimpered and whined so much. But what did a man do when he was without a gun? He hadn't set a rabbit snare for nearly twenty-five years, and besides, he hadn't seen sign of a rabbit or anything in the last two days.

He wondered how some of those old mountain men got along. They had some tricks of staying alive, some way to get food into their bellies even when there apparently wasn't anything to eat.

Kill the horse? Oh, that would be a stupid thing to do. Maybe bleed him a little; there was nourishment in blood. Then he rejected that because he'd heard once that it made a man sick. He couldn't afford to get sick. He'd seen some bird tracks in the snow, but how could a man catch a bird? Throw a stick at it?

He tried to dredge up something from all the bunkhouse talk he'd heard about just how long a person could go without eating. A couple of weeks? The thought sent a newer, sharper agony through his stomach. No man could live that long without food, and not endure the hunger pains. And the boy couldn't go on this way. Another day and he'd be howling all the time.

And I'll be howling right with him, Gannon thought.

Toward morning, Gannon climbed into the rocks to gather some dry brush. The wind was still strong and the promise of snow was raw in the air. No sign of daylight yet, but it was coming. A faint blush of light marked the horizon.

He could see a far piece across the broad valley floor. It seemed to grow broader as they had moved along the length of it. Probably a river down there somewhere, and Gannon hoped there was thick ice on it. Then he saw a wink of light out there against the backdrop of predawn darkness; it looked like a star brought down to earth. Only he knew it wasn't. Somebody had got out of a warm bed and lit the lamp before making the morning fire, and he thought it was the finest sight he had ever seen. Gannon stood there and watched the light, and the dawn came and the light did not shine so brightly; finally he could not see it at all.

He hurried down to their bare camp and woke the boy. 'Up, Beans! Up! Let's go!'

'I'm awful hungry.'

'We'll eat today,' Gannon said and put him on the horse. Before he mounted, he looked at the ground where the snow was pawed away, exposing dried grass. It was lucky, he guessed, to be a horse.

There wasn't much go left in the animal, and Gannon had to push back the impulse to press him regardless. No use killing the animal five miles from the place. A man could starve on a doorstep just as easily as he could in the middle of a desert.

A feeling came to him that he should spend

more time watching his back trail, and Gannon began to look back. He kept that up all morning, and around noon he thought he saw something but he couldn't be sure. The place in the valley was getting bigger all the time, but Gannon knew that if he hadn't seen the lamp go on he'd have missed it, because it blended so well with the land. A low soddy, or a log house, with a barn and corral; he estimated that he was yet four miles away, or maybe a little less.

The looks behind told him that he was going to have company; six Apaches rode in a close knot, and showed every sign of picking up on him before he could reach shelter.

Gannon figured then that if the horse had anything left, this was the time to run it out of him. It would probably kill the animal and he was sorry about that, but he had no choice.

He spurred the horse into a dead run and didn't look back now; he didn't have time for it, and didn't care either. This was the last shot in the carbine, and if he didn't make it, he just didn't make it. Looking back to see death coming wouldn't change anything.

Less than half a mile from the ranch house, the horse stumbled and they both went off into a loose rolling fall. Beans could never keep up, Gannon knew, and hoisted him to his back, then ran on, his heart pumping up the last bit of strength into his legs.

He thought he heard horses behind him, but he couldn't be sure; the blood was a roar in his ears, and his vision smeared over so that everything got a little hazy. Then he heard a .50 caliber Sharps boom and from behind came one long yell of disappointment, and the sound of horses faded.

Gannon staggered into the yard and just sprawled out. The cabin door opened and three men came out. One of them was very tall and he wore a beard so long that the end of it was tucked into the collar of his underwear. The other two were younger, with the same eyes, the same flat way of looking at a man.

Then the tall man said, 'Ruben, Sam, take 'em inside.' He stood there, squinting at the retreating Apaches, then he laughed hollowly and went in the cabin.

The heat was a pain to Charlie Gannon and he lay gasping on the floor, his knees drawn up to his chest. 'He's got a cramp, Pa,' one of the young men said.

'From that run, I guess. Get the horse linament.'

They popped the boy into a tub of hot water and made him sit there howling because it hurt. Gannon was stripped, rubbed down with linament, and his hands were greased and bandaged. A cot was brought in from somewhere out back and set up in the main living room. After he was placed on it, he had a hard time to keep from just falling off into a vast sea of comfort.

The old man came over, his pipe clenched

between his teeth. 'How long since you ate?'

'Couple days. No, three,' Gannon said. 'Who're you?'

'Kertcher. My boys, Rube and Sam. Fix some broth, boys. That will do for a starter.' He took Beans out of the tub and dried him with a towel. 'Why, you're a white one! Thought you was Mex or something with all that dirt on you.'

'My mum's a Mormon,' Beans said.

Kertcher grinned. 'Be that so? Mine was Episcopalian.' He smacked him smartly on the round bottom. 'My boys will fetch you blankets. Curl up by the fire there. Let your pappy have the bed.' Then he turned back to Gannon. 'The young ones are tough; they spring back quick. A little something in his belly and he'll be chasin' deer tomorrow.'

The two Kertcher boys made some broth, which tasted like potato soup, but Gannon thought it was the best he'd ever eaten. With his hands all bandaged up, they had to feed him, but he was too burned out to feel embarrassed about it.

They let him sleep until he wanted to wake up, and it was dark when he did. He lay there, letting the lamplight make his eyelids red, then he opened them and looked around the room. Ruben was cleaning the table of supper dishes, and he put them down and got out a clean plate.

'It's stew,' he said, bringing it over to the cot.

Gannon sat up, took the spoon in his fist, and made out all right by himself.

Kertcher sat at the table, smoking his pipe. 'The boy says you ain't his pap.'

'That's right,' Gannon said. 'It's a long story.'

The old man shrugged to say that he didn't care one way or another. Outside the wind pushed at the walls and Kertcher said, 'You found us just in time. It's a whizzer out there. But the Apaches will make out all right, damn 'em. Been killin' 'em for nearly twenty years now. Buried a wife, three sons and a daughter. They buried ten times that many.'

'If it's that bad, why stay?' Gannon asked.

'Because what's mine is mine,' Kertcher said flatly. 'You know, man. You got the boy back, didn't you?'

'Is it the same?'

'Hell, yes, it's the same. For some of us, everything comes hard. We've got to understand it. Live with it. Now eat your stew. There's more if you're still hungry.'

CHAPTER FOURTEEN

For the two horses and supplies, Charlie Gannon insisted on giving his note to Kertcher; Gannon would redeem it in the spring, by returning the horses and paying for the supplies, or paying for everything. Kertcher insisted that this wasn't necessary, but Gannon wouldn't be argued out of his way.

Neither could he be persuaded to remain longer; he considered six days more than an imposition on Kertcher's hospitality. And he was feeling better, his wrists were healing nicely, and his fingers were only sore because of the peeling.

With the storm over and a heavy blanket of snow on the ground, Gannon knew traveling would be difficult, but it would also be difficult for the Indians, so much so that they might not consider one man and a boy worth the trouble of killing. The two Kertcher boys sorted through some of the things they kept in trunks, clothes belonging to their own brothers, now dead, and Beans was outfitted in odd-sized shirts and pants and a coat two times too large for him.

Gannon spent one whole morning in the barn, loading the pack horse. Kertcher came out to lend a hand.

'Keep in the valley for another forty–fifty miles,' Kertcher said, 'and you'll run smack dab into the monument country.' He took off his mittens to fill his pipe. 'It'll take you a week to ten days, Gannon. You sure you don't want to wait until spring?'

'I can't,' Gannon said. He made a final knot, tested the pack, then blew on his hands to warm them. 'I've got to get the boy back to her,

Kertcher.'

The old man frowned and drew noisily on his pipe. 'I've been trying not to stick my nose in your business, Gannon. But the older a man gets, the more pokey he becomes. Gets so he can't stand it.' He looked at Gannon and grinned behind his beard. 'Which is it now? You want to get the boy back, or get yourself back?'

'The boy—now,' Gannon said. He gave Kertcher a careful, serious study, then said, 'What does a man do when he finds out he ain't much at all?'

'Depends on what he found out.'

'There was a couple of times there when I wanted to cut out for myself and leave the boy,' Gannon said. 'I had all the pretty lies figured out too, so I'd look like I'd tried real hard.' He made a movement with his mouth, as though he had bitten into something bitter. 'I can't go back and pretend to her that it don't make a difference, that it didn't happen.' He tapped himself on the chest. 'I was going to leave that boy behind, Kertcher. Don't you think I'll remember that every time I look at him, or her?'

'So you remember it,' Kertcher said. 'Why don't you get a stick and whip yourself with it every day?'

Gannon was insulted. 'What kind of a fool thing is that to say?'

'What's foolish about it?' Kertcher wanted

229

to know. 'A man steps out on his wife, and regrets it. Or he kills another because he did somethin' stupid. A thing bad like that is over and it's done. Let it be that way.' He paused a moment. 'I guess you'll tell her.'

'Yes, I'll tell her,' Gannon said.

The Kertcher boys came out of the house, and Ruben carried Beans on his shoulders. Sam had a sack of food and a single-barreled shotgun. When they reached the barn, he gave the gun to Gannon, saying, 'I'd like to let you have a rifle, but Rube broke the firing pin on his, so all we've got left is a buffalo gun and this spare ten-gauge.' He handed over a sack of shells. 'There's some small-game shot in there and a dozen double 00 buck, for something Indian-size.'

'I've had enough of Indians,' Gannon said. He gave the boy a playful thump. 'Ready to light out?'

'Yup,' Beans said. He gave each one of the Kertchers a hug in turn, then Gannon shook hands and stepped into the saddle. He reached around the boy to take the reins, looked once at the pack horse, then spoke to the Kertchers.

'Likely it'll be spring before I can get these horses back to you.'

'We'll see you then,' Kertcher said. 'Take care, Gannon. Travel easy. You got time now.'

'I guess,' Gannon said.

Then he rode from the yard, trying to stay in the blow fallows between the deeper drifts.

A six-man military detail took the Benson women home, then returned to Jenny Regan's place. Captain Anders went to the house and knocked; Louise Benson opened the door. He stepped inside, took off his gloves and cape and moved nearer the stove where Jenny was fixing the noon meal. She no longer wore the heavy bandage around her head, although the wound was still healing.

'My rations are about gone,' he said. 'We've got enough to make the post without turning Apache and eating our horses.'

'Paul, you've extended more than military aid,' Jenny said.

Anders smiled. 'That's the first time you've ever used my name, Jenny. Somehow it marks a milestone, but of what I'm not exactly sure. I'm sorry Charlie Gannon isn't back. And I'd like to give you some assurance, but he's been gone a long time now and—'

'You don't have to explain it,' she said quickly. 'Thank you for everything.'

He nodded. 'Clayton will be better off here than if we took him back to the post. If I can, I'll try to get the surgeon to come along on the next patrol, although that may not be for a month or so. Just keep the wound clean and draining. And give him one of those pills when the pain gets bad. I've been warned they're

231

habit-forming, so be careful with them.' He twirled his hat in his hands. 'Damn it, Jenny, I wish there was someth—'

'There isn't,' she said.

'Well, you can't stay here alone now,' Anders said.

'I'll wait until spring,' Jenny said. 'That's not too long.'

Anders' glance touched Louise Benson. 'I talked to your father. He'll come after you when it thaws. Well, I guess I'd better say good-bye to Ben. Been some winter, hasn't it?'

'Yes, some winter,' Jenny said.

Going into the bedroom, Anders closed the door. Then he sat down by the bed. 'The army's going to get worried about me,' Anders said. 'I don't like long good-byes, do you?' He reached out and took Clayton's good hand, then his manner turned serious. 'We work damned hard, Ben, but do any of us really get what we want?'

'I don't even know what I want,' Clayton said. 'Once it was fun I wanted, but now it's—well, I don't know if I can lead her life, Captain.'

'Give it a try. Ben, I saw her face when she looked at you, so I plastered up that arm bent so it would be just right for pitching hay. Don't make me out a wrong guesser now.'

Clayton laughed. 'You're a hell of a joker.' Then his smile faded. 'Nothing from Charlie, huh?' Anders shook his head. 'You suppose the Indians got him?'

'Indians, winter, a man's one foolish mistake—' He shrugged his lean shoulders. 'You'll make it without Charlie now. If he walked in that door tomorrow, there wouldn't be anything the same.' He got up and pulled on his gloves. 'If you want, we'll take those horses back for you; they'll be too much to hand feed with you flat on your back. I'll have your account credited with the paymaster.'

'Thanks,' Ben Clayton said. 'With the Kerry bunch gone—'

'Yes,' Anders said regretfully. 'We'd buy about a hundred and fifty a year. Well, we'll see how you make out with the arm. If there's any movement in the fingers—'

He let the rest hang there, as it would have to hang for months. Again he shook Clayton's hand, then turned and went out. He started for the door, then stopped and turned to Louise Benson. 'Are you going to marry him? Good. Then don't make a hay-shaker out of him.'

'I—I don't know what you mean.'

'I mean, he's a man. Let him be one. Good-bye, ladies.'

They got their coats and went outside to watch the army leave. A detail of men fought Clayton's horses, roped them in strings, then began the drive back. Anders' offer to take the horses along just wasn't pure generosity; he used them, roped four abreast, to break trail, and by rotating the strings, he would give them

233

a chance to rest on the move and at the same time make a rapid march back to Fort Defiance.

After they were gone, Jenny Regan found little time in which to think about how lonely she was, and how many long winters were ahead of her. The stock had to be fed and taken care of and Ben Clayton occupied most of Louise's time. In the evenings they tried to mend what damage they could, although neither were carpenters.

After the sixth day, Ben insisted on getting up and they didn't argue with him; they didn't have to, for twenty minutes on his feet exhausted him and he gladly went to bed. But he was stubborn about it and kept stretching the time, until he could stay up for an hour or so without keeling over. And he wanted to do what he could, help with the meals or the cleaning and dishes.

He built a fire outside one day so Jenny and Louise could wash the clothes. But they had to be taken into the house to be hung up to dry, and that night the place was damp and smelled strongly of wet woolens.

Ben began to spend more time outside, sometimes half a day at a time. He insisted on doing the outside chores, although it took him twice as long.

One day he came tromping into the kitchen at noon-time, and he didn't even bother to kick the snow from his boots. Jenny Regan was going to say something about it but his expression held her back.

'You want to see somethin'?' Clayton asked. 'Come on outside.'

He took her arm and walked her around the side of the house to where they had a clear view along the snow-covered canyon floor. He had to point before her eyes caught sight of the two horses, and then she said, 'Oooohhh,' explosively, and began to run through the snow. Her long dress slowed her, so she hoisted it. She fell a few times but got up and kept on running.

Louise came out and said, 'What is it, Ben?'

'Lost lambs,' Clayton said, and put his arm around her without thinking. She stiffened in surprise, then leaned against him and they watched Jenny Regan run.

They could hear Beans shouting, 'Mum! Mum!' Then he jumped down off the horse and almost disappeared in the deeper drifts. He half ran, half jumped, bobbing in and out of sight, then they met and Jenny scooped him in her arms and held him. Gannon came on as though his need to hurry was over. He dismounted, took the boy from Jenny, and put him on top of the pack-horse. Then he lifted her to the saddle and came on to the house.

Jenny was laughing and crying at the same time when Gannon let her off near the door. The boy ran and hugged Ben Clayton around the legs.

Gannon acted as though he wasn't going to get down, then he swung a leg over and stepped off. A good growth of beard covered his face and when he looked at Ben Clayton, his eyes seemed more tired, as though the end of something was in sight and he wasn't looking forward to it.

His eyebrows lifted when he looked at Clayton's arm. Ben smiled and said, 'The Kerry bunch and I had an argument.'

'Bad?' Gannon asked.

'The elbow's gone.' Then he gave Gannon a push, saying, 'Go on in, Charlie. I'll take care of the horse.'

'I'll help you,' Louise said and dashed in for her coat.

Beans ran in to see if there were any cookies in the jar and Jenny stood in the doorway, smiling and drying her eyes. 'Charlie, aren't you going to come in?' She reached out and he came to her and they went on inside; he closed the door and leaned against it. 'Let me take your coat.' She collected the things as he shed them and put them on wall pegs.

'Are you all right, Jenny?'

'I'm fine, now,' she said. 'Charlie, sit down.' She moved a box away from the table for him, then went to the coffee pot and brought back a steaming cup.

Beans deserted the empty cookie crock and said, 'I'm hungry, Mum.'

'I'll fix you something soon,' she said. 'Go

see what Ben and Louise are doing.' The boy grabbed his coat and ran out and Jenny sat down across from Gannon. 'You look so tired, Charlie.'

'Will Ben's arm be any good?' She shook her head slowly. 'Never?' He didn't seem able to believe it.

'He won't be able to move it.' Then she reached out and took his hands, and bit her lip at the way the frost-bite had made them peel. 'Will you tell me about it, Charlie?'

'Shanti went to the Apaches with him,' Gannon said. 'Say, could you heat some water so I could shave off this brush?' She got up and slid the teakettle on the hot part of the stove while he went on talking. 'I killed Shanti. Three or four others too.' He shook his head, not wanting to say any more about it.

Ben and Louise came back with the boy while he was lathering his face, and Ben laughed. 'You goin' to come out behind that so we can look at you?' He shook out his tobacco and rolled a cigaret with his good hand, a trick he had patiently practiced. 'The next time you go someplace, don't stay so long, huh?'

Gannon glanced sharply at him, and Louise caught her breath. 'Ben, what's got into you?'

'Let him alone,' Gannon said. 'He's feeling sassy. I suppose you let the Kerry bunch steal our horses?'

'Nope. Captain Anders drove them back to the post. He'll credit our account.'

'You really got yourself gimped up, didn't you?'

Ben Clayton shrugged. 'I can still lick you with one hand.'

'Ben!' Louise snapped.

Gannon held up his hand and she fell silent. 'Aren't you going to get mad, Ben?'

'No, why should I?' He came to the table and leaned his hand against it so he could look Gannon in the eye. 'Who the hell needs you anyway? I don't.'

'Well ain't we got big britches?' Gannon said. He went on shaving and when he was through, he wiped his face with a towel. Carefully he folded the razor, then he leaned back and examined Ben Clayton. 'Somehow you ain't the same, Ben. I like you better now. I guess you could lick me with one hand.' His glance touched Louise Benson. 'The way you keep looking at him worries me some. What's your pa going to say about it?'

'I don't care what he says,' Louise told him.

Charlie Gannon shrugged. 'Then there's nothing much he can do. You going to be a farmer, Ben?'

'If I have to.' He sat down across from Gannon, his eyes brightening with enthusiasm. 'Anders told me that the army buys about a hundred and fifty horses a year, Charlie. Hell, we ought to be able to handle that. If I've got any use of my fingers when this heals, we could make out fine.'

'What makes you think I want to?' Gannon asked. He spread his hands, then waved them briefly and let them drop into his lap. 'You don't have to hold me up any longer, Ben.'

Clayton frowned. 'What's eating you anyway?' Then he turned to Jenny Regan. 'Why don't you two take the boy and go look at the cow? I'm going to start cussing in a minute and I don't want to have to apologize for it later.'

Louise said, 'Come on, Jenny.'

But Jenny Regan kept looking at Gannon. 'Charlie, what's the matter?'

Louise took her arm. 'Come on. Ben knows best.'

They went out and Clayton waited a moment before speaking. 'I don't know what's galling you, Charlie; I sure never saw you feeling this sorry for yourself before.' He raised the bullet-fractured arm. 'You think I like this? I almost puked when Mrs. Benson made me look at it. But I got it, Charlie. Damn it, it's mine and I'm going to live with it and there ain't going to be any bawling about it either.' He lowered his voice. 'Charlie, we're just a couple of dumb men trying to live, to get along the best we can. Maybe it isn't what we want. Maybe we'll end up a couple of nothings, but hell, we've got to lean, Charlie. We all lean on each other. If we didn't the world would fall down. Half of the money is yours, Charlie. We were partners. In the spring, when it starts to

239

thaw, I thought I'd try to build across the valley a few miles. Maybe my house will have crooked walls and a roof that leaks because I'm a sloppy carpenter, but I'm going to build it anyway and put pans out when it rains to catch the water. Don't I make sense to you, Charlie?'

'You make a lot of sense, Ben.'

'Then what's wrong?'

Gannon got up and walked around the room, looking at the boarded-up windows with old quilts tacked in place to hold back the cold. 'The place got shot up a little, didn't it?'

'Yeah, but what's that got to do with it?'

He shrugged. 'I've got to tell Jenny the truth, Ben. I was going to run and leave the kid behind.' He waited for Clayton to speak, then turned and looked at him to see why he didn't. Clayton was making a one-handed cigaret, and Gannon said, 'Didn't you hear me?'

'Sure, I heard you. So what do you want me to say?'

'Tell me what kind of a man I am.'

'You're not as good as you always thought you were,' Clayton said. 'It comes as a surprise to all of us. What are you going to do, make Jenny cry some more because you were yellow for a couple of minutes?' He laughed without humor. 'You should have seen me the night the Kerry bunch hit this place and I found out Mrs. Benson burned my rifle. I looked like a dandelion out there in the snow.' He got up and threw his cigaret in the stove. Then he faced Gannon. 'Why the hell don't you go out there to Jenny and kiss her? And if you open your mouth about wanting to leave the boy behind, I'll beat your head off. You never could fight anyway.'

Gannon thought about this for a time, then he stepped to the door. When his hand touched the latch, he stopped and said, 'Ben, we're still partners?'

'You'll never get rid of me,' Ben Clayton said. 'I'll help you build a new barn in the spring if you'll give me a hand with my place.'

'Sort of a you-scrub-my-back, I'll-scrub-yours?'

Clayton grinned. 'Why not, Charlie? We'll be the cleanest two bums in the country.' Then he nodded toward the back of the yard. 'Ain't you kept her waiting long enough?'

'I have at that,' Gannon said, and stepped outside.

And Ben Clayton heard him calling to her before he reached the corral.

We hope you have enjoyed this Large Print book. Other Chivers Press or G.K. Hall & Co. Large Print books are available at your library or directly from the publishers.

For more information about current and forthcoming titles, please call or write, without obligation, to:

Chivers Press Limited
Windsor Bridge Road
Bath BA2 3AX
England
Tel. (01225) 335336

OR

G.K. Hall & Co.
P.O. Box 159
Thorndike, Maine 04986
USA
Tel. (800) 223-2336

All our Large Print titles are designed for easy reading, and all our books are made to last.